Two novellas and three short stories comprise this steamy-hot collection of big and small endowed muscle erotica. Follow bodybuilder Shamus Little on a journey from his late teens to middle age as he learns how to use his best asset.

LITTLE SHAMUS is an autobiographical account of a bodybuilder's physical and sexual awakening. With his coach and fellow bodybuilders, Shamus explores the limits of pain, pleasure, and anatomy.

MUSCLE BEACH picks up where Little Shamus leaves off. The young bodybuilder meets his match and proves his gluteus maximus can take it like a winner.

THE SPOTTER is a brief account of a gym pickup. It is a very early story about body modification with silicone, too.

DIRTY COP brings Shamus in contact with two cops, Rocco and Ash, who partake in all the pleasures the little bodybuilder has to offer.

HARDHATS AND NIGHTSTICKS follows the life of Shane Biggars, a very well-endowed construction worker who eventually meets cops Ash and Rocco, then Shamus. His life gets better when he and Shamus work together to build furntiure and a perfect union.

MUSCLE BOTTOM

PETER SCHUTES

CONTENTS

FOREWORD

Muscle Bottom is a collection of short stories and novellas that center around Shamus Little, a short, stocky bodybuilder with an extraordinary ability to please men of all sizes. Bodybuilding is a frequent theme in Peter Schutes's work. The cult of muscle was seductive. Lifting weights allowed men to transform their size and shape. It lends itself perfectly to the themes of his work.

Peter Schutes frequented Muscle Beach from the 1950s until he died in 1981. He confided to his friend and protégé Adam Maxwell Bigglesworth that bodybuilders were his weakness. He so rarely found a partner who could handle him. Bodybuilders are a rare breed. They learn to push through pain. Some even end up enjoying it.

Peter never admitted whether Shamus Little was a real weightlifter from Muscle Beach. When we asked Adam, he said there were several men in his life like Shamus Little. Adam's best guess is that Shamus was an amalgam of several lovers, most of whom never made it into his autobiography.

This is the complete collection of Shamus stories. There are two novellas and three short stories. According to some notes we found paper-clipped to the text, Peter wrote "Little Shamus" in an autobiographical style, using coarse language and intentionally dumbing down his sentences to try and understand what it might be like to "think with one's body." He also said, "The pretense of writing as an intellectually inferior man is difficult and downright obnoxious. I had to give it up in favor of a more literate presentation."

The psychological underpinnings are apparent. Peter often confided to anyone who would listen that he wanted to know what it would be like to be "little." *Little Shamus* is one of several stories Peter told from the point of view of a bottom struggling to overcome the shame of his miniscule endowment. Peter had a love/hate relationship with his monstrous size. He found no sympathy. Society might pity the man who was too small, but nobody seemed to believe that being too big was a genuine problem. American society, puritanical and prude, all but refused to acknowledge that men even have a penis. Having a large one garnered no sympathy and was a forbidden topic of conversation at every dinner party.

The three short stories progress through time. *Muscle Beach* picks up right where Little Shamus left off. Both would take place in 1957, the year that Muscle Beach closed and moved from Santa Monica to Venice. We fast forward to the mid-1960s for *The Spotter*, a story set at Joe Gold's first gym in Venice, California. *Dirty Cop* takes place perhaps five years later. Shamus has taken a wayward path with drugs and steroids and nearly pays the consequences. As a fan of muscles and bodybuilding, Peter likely saw the dark changes in the physical culture community as the societal changes of the late 1960s gave way to the decadent 1970s.

Hardhats and Nightsticks tacks on a happy ending to Shamus's story. It focuses on Shane Biggars, the construction worker, but Shamus makes an appearance that ultimately steals the show. Peter released all of these stories at different times, but we put them together in the chronological order that made the most sense. We hope you'll enjoy the adventures of Little Shamus as he discovers the joys of having, building, and loving his body.

—Your Friends at Peter Schutes Publishing

LITTLE SHAMUS

SCHOOL WAS HARD

My name is Shamus Little, and I love two things: bodybuilding and sex. Lifting weights was my first love, but I dig men even more. I'm not ashamed to admit it. This is the story of how I ended up like this.

I ain't the brightest bulb in the bunch. School was hard. Math didn't make no sense, and I already speak English, so why did I have to learn to write it? I got good at writing, but it took a while. What I did good was recess. That was when we got to play ball or run around the track. I got Satisfactory in Math, English, and Penmanship but Excellent in Physical Activity. Later, when I went to Berendo Middle School in Los Angeles, I got all A's in P.E. I was short but fast and limber. I even did better than almost everybody in Basketball! But gymnastics was my favorite. I could do the splits since I was a kid, and it didn't take much to learn to tumble. I had a tight little body and lots of upper body strength.

In my Junior year at Belmont High School, they installed a weight room. It was a brand-new idea. Jack LaLanne and those Hercules and Tarzan movies convinced Coach Hurley that it was time to teach kids how to be strong. He called us a bunch of pussies, and most of the kids didn't want to do it, but I did. I saw those barbells and thought, "This is what I'm supposed to be doing."

From the minute I started lifting, my body grew. By senior year, I looked better than Steve Reeves, though maybe not as tall. And maybe not as big down there.

Yeah, I got a little dick. So, what? My chest and legs are so hot the guys (and girls) never even look there. And my ass is big enough to set a drink on it. I didn't want sex with anybody, boy or girl, until my last semester of high school. I'd stayed back a year, so I was nineteen. Yeah, okay, a virgin at nineteen, but with my little dick, I didn't want nobody seeing it or touching it. Turns out, they didn't really care. Girls were too needy. I didn't know why I didn't like them until Coach Hurley showed me the way.

One day, I was doing squats, and I seen Coach Hurley standing in the doorway watching me. He was looking at my legs, I figured. But he wasn't.

He said, "Shamus, after this, come see me in my office."

I thought I was in trouble, but when he smiled, I felt something funny going on in my gut.

"Hey Coach, what's up?"

He said, "I've been watching you, and I think you're a natural. You have great form, and nearly every muscle shows itself as you move. Do you know how special that is?"

I shook my head.

"Well, Shamus, it's pretty damn special. There's competitions for this stuff out in Santa Monica. You heard of Muscle Beach?"

"No, sir."

The coach grinned and leaned forward, looking me straight in the eyes. "I think you should enter one of those contests." Then he put his hand on my forearm. I thought it was weird, but it felt good. He squeezed it.

"Look at you. Barely five feet tall and 150 pounds of muscle. You're a real lady killer, I bet."

I shrugged. "Nah, I don't have a girlfriend or nothin'."

Then the coach licked his lips. He took out a measuring tape. "Let's see how big you are."

I immediately thought of my little dick, even though I knew he meant something else. He was wearing gray sweatpants. When he stood up, I could see he had a hard-on. It wasn't big, not like the kind I like now, but it was obvious.

He stood close to me while he measured my neck, chest, shoulders, biceps, and waist. When he got to my thighs, he brushed against my crotch. I was hard, but he'd never know it. I was relieved I was so small just then because I was ashamed of how much I liked him touching me. Then he said something.

"It's okay. Not everyone has a big one. It makes your legs stand out."

I must have been beet red because my face was burning. After Coach did my thighs, he went to my hips and ass. He whistled.

"Shoot, that's nice."

I wasn't sure what he meant. Now he was rubbing his crotch and looking at me like a fried chicken dinner.

"You don't have a girlfriend. Do you like men?"

"No!" I was quick to say it because it meant I was a faggot, and I didn't realize it until just that second. I didn't want him to know.

"Are you sure? It's okay if you do. I like men."

"Y-you're a faggot?"

The coach smacked my leg hard. "I'm not a faggot, Shamus. I appreciate a good body on anyone. But yours is beyond perfect. He put a hand on my ass and started rubbing it. My gym shorts got wet.

"So you don't have sex with men, right?" I was hardly ever scared, but this had me freaking out.

"Oh, I do. Women, too. I have kids, Shamus. But that doesn't mean I don't like to play around with guys. I'm bisexual."

I was curious. "Do you want to have sex with me?" I meant it one way, but it came out another.

"I thought you'd never ask." He pulled down his sweats, and his boner popped out. It was probably just five inches, but compared to my little pecker, it was huge. I didn't know what I was supposed to do with it at first. He stepped forward and brushed it against my lips. I guess I'd been dreaming about something like this. My body was shaking; I was so scared. I put my hand around it. It felt amazing to pull on it. When I played with myself, it was just my thumb and finger. I used my whole hand on Coach Hurley.

I pulled on it for a couple of minutes. The Coach moaned and shifted around a lot.

"Do you want to suck it?" He put a hand behind my ear and gently pulled me closer. I could see it was leaking the same stuff I did. That clear, drippy shit. I didn't think; I just licked it up. It tasted way better than I thought it would. The coach's legs shook.

"Suck it, son."

I didn't have no father, and when he called me son, I felt like some missing piece just fell into place. I opened my mouth and wrapped it around the tip of his dick. He pulled me closer by the ear, and it slipped into my mouth. When he reached close to the end, I felt like puking. He stopped right there, letting me hurl a few times.

"It'll stop, son. Just control it, like you do when you're releasing a dumbbell. Just nice and slow, that's it."

My eyes were watering. He pushed all the way in and tickled my tonsils. Then he put both hands behind my head and pulled me real close so my nose was buried in his pubic hair. Then he humped my face.

"Oh, Shamus, you're a natural at this, too."

I felt proud. The coach appreciated me like a son. I didn't know why I needed that so bad. But I did. I tasted more of that sticky stuff, and it made my little pee pee drool. I fingered it while I sucked the coach's dick. I'd played with myself before but didn't know about coming yet. I just liked how it felt and then quit. I never realized there was more. With that dick in my mouth, I felt something building inside me. The coach started to breathe faster, and I could tell he was building up, too.

"Oh fuck, Shamus, you're gonna make me come." There was that word. And hearing it made my dick start to throb. The coach's dick was bigger than ever. It fit in my mouth, but I could feel it pulsing against my lips. He grabbed me again and held himself inside, at the back of my mouth.

"Oh shit, oh shit!" Then I felt it, the warm blast of come filling my mouth.

I couldn't say nothing, so I just hummed and breathed hard through my nose. That building sensation felt so weird, then it went off the chart. I thought I peed my shorts, but it was thick and goopy, just like the coach. That was the first time I ever came.

When the coach stepped back, his drippy cock hit my chin and then landed on his balls. He got out a towel and wiped it off. Then he lifted me up and kissed me, letting his tongue taste some of his own jizz. His mustache tickled my nose, just like his pubes had done. I liked it when he kissed me like that. It was my first kiss, and it came after my first time sucking dick!

"You're a good little cocksucker, son. Real good."

I smiled. "Thank you, sir."

2

TRYING SOMETHING NEW

After that day, I stayed late every afternoon and sucked the coach's dick. He always appreciated it. One day, he pulled out early, still rock hard. I liked how it looked when it stood up off his balls. Mine was sort of buried and didn't stick out none.

"Shamus, I want to teach you something. You want to learn a new technique?"

Of course, I did. I nodded hard.

"Good. This might hurt a little at first, but I promise me you'll beg me for more when it's over." He put a hand on my ass and rubbed it. "Oh man, you got a sweet ass."

He licked his finger, then stuck it down my shorts. I was wearing a jockstrap, so his finger slipped right between my two butt cheeks. They were solid steel. His wet finger poked my asshole.

"Did you know that men have pussies?"

I laughed. "No, we don't! You're crazy."

He pushed his fingertip into my shitter. "See, right there."

"That's where shit comes out. My asshole."

The coach smiled at me. "Yeah, but stuff can go in, too." He pushed, and I felt the first knuckle as it slipped past the exit door. It felt awful. It stung a little.

But when he pulled it back out, it felt good, like when you finish a shit.

"How did that feel?"

I shrugged. "It didn't feel good until you took it out."

"If I go further, it will feel even better when I take it out, right? Just like how you feel good after you put down a barbell after a chest press."

I could relate to that. The pushing never felt good, and controlled release didn't either, but when you set those weights on the rack saddle, you felt high.

"When I push my finger in, pretend you're lifting, then when I pull it out, pretend you set them down."

He pushed his whole finger inside. I hated it. His fingers were thin, but it still felt like he was breaking some law of nature doing that. When he pulled it out, I shivered. That felt fucking great. The next time he pushed in, he pressed on a spot in my ass I never even knew about. It was like taking three shits in a row. I couldn't help it; my hips bucked.

"Ah, see, that's the best part. That's why it's a pussy, son." As he said it, he pulled the finger out almost the whole way, then slipped it back in. It burned. The spit wasn't helping no more.

He took it out again. He pulled a tub of Vaseline from the drawer and pulled out a glob with two fingers. He spat on it.

"Spread your cheeks, son."

I did what he told me. He wiped some on my hole, then stuck in one finger, this time the middle one. It went right in. Each time he did it, he pressed on that spot, and my little dick started to drool.

"Feels good now, doesn't it?"

Right when I nodded, he stuck in both fingers. I jumped. I saw stars. But he kept sliding in, pressing that button, and sliding out. Soon, it felt good again. Then he twisted his fingers and spread them apart a little.

Then a little more, still sliding in and out, pushing that button. I moaned.

"See, it's a pussy."

He pulled his fingers out. "I guess that's enough, right?"

He watched my face. I was disappointed.

Coach watched my face. "We can go farther if you want."

"M-more fingers?"

He nodded.

I said, "Yeah, that'd be cool."

The third finger didn't hurt. I guess he'd stretched me enough.

"Lay down on that bench and put your legs up."

I was on my back, half his hand inside me. He added a fourth finger and slid in so the web between his thumb and finger tickled my asshole.

"Okay, you're ready."

He pulled down his pants and jerked his cock a few times. It was slick with Vaseline. He spat in his palm and rubbed some more.

"What are you doing?"

"Hush, Shamus. You're gonna love it."

And I did. Coach held my legs, so my ass was in the air and set them on his shoulders. He walked forward until his dick slipped between my butt cheeks and tapped the hole.

"Breathe out, and push like you're taking a shit." He pushed at the same time and slipped inside me. It hurt like a motherfucker, but he waited. "You ready?"

I nodded. I knew dicks went in pussies, so I should have expected this. Still, it made me feel a little less of a man. I felt girly. But I didn't care because it felt so fucking good. The coach fucked me good. I felt his dick slipping and sliding around in there. It was thick enough that it pushed on that button each time it went in. It felt sort of like that feeling you get right before you sneeze but don't quite.

Coach Hurley looked in my eyes. "Feels good, right?"

I couldn't really talk, so I just nodded.

"I'm going slow now. Want me to go faster?"

"Yes, sir."

He sped up, and my eyes rolled up in my head. I felt his mustache on my mouth, and his tongue went inside. I licked his tongue like I had after all those times I'd sucked his dick. He made this deep sound, like a grunt. I tried to do the same, but it sounded like a girl at the grocery store throwing a tantrum. He was making me a girl! And fuck if I didn't love it. Then I surprised myself. I shot a load up against the coach's furry belly.

He pulled away from the kiss. "Oh, Shamus, I made you come! Like a girl."

I blushed. "I'm a man. I'm a man." I kept saying it in my head because it felt like I was turning into a girl, not a dude. Something was slipping out of my hands, like a dumbbell dropping on the gym floor. I started to cry like a little bitch.

The coach didn't stop, but he talked between thrusts. "Shamus. Are. You. Okay?"

I shook my head. The coach stopped.

"Am I hurting you?"

"NO. Keep fucking me! We can talk after." I didn't want the fucking to ever stop. I could have stayed like that with Coach Hurley for the rest of my life. Or at least it felt like it. I didn't feel any pain at all; it was pure pleasure. I felt another wave building in me, making me buck and thrash. The Coach's short dick popped out of me, but he stuck it right back in and kept plugging away.

I wanted him to go deeper but didn't think he could. I grabbed his hairy ass and pulled it close so he was as deep as possible. He set down one leg and rolled me onto my side. Suddenly, his pubes were pushing past my butt cheeks, and his hips landed on my hole. It was deeper. I kept bucking, but now he didn't fall out.

"You like it deep?" The coach's sweat fell on my face.

"Yeah."

"This is as far as I go. Is it enough?"

I nodded, but part of me wanted more. I said, "Just keep doing it hard like that."

He didn't need another invitation. He just pounded me so hard that I slid along the bench. He grabbed my shoulders to keep me close. He was moving so fast that his body's bottom half was blurry.

"Oh, shit, son. Here I come!"

Just hearing the words made me squirt another load. Then Coach Hurley filled my ass with come and collapsed on top of me. His breath was hot against my earlobes. He kissed me hard. His dick got soft and slipped out. I felt a trickle of sperm dribbling out of my asshole, making the bench dirty.

After we caught our breath, he sat up.

"What did you want to talk about, son? I could see something was bothering you."

I shrugged. "It's hard to talk about. I just...I felt weird. You know?"

The coach frowned. "It didn't feel good?"

"Oh, no! It felt fucking great. I just felt, well, I dunno."

The coach put a reassuring hand on my shoulder. "You can say it, whatever's bothering you."

I couldn't hold back no more. "I felt like a girl."

Coach Hurley laughed. Not in a way that hurt. It was the kind of laugh that made you feel special. I guess I felt a father's love just then.

"Shamus, you're more of a man when you do that. No woman gets off like a man. I know I said you were coming like a girl, but that was the wrong words. You were coming because you're so good at this. Your pussy, your ass, it's built right for fucking."

That helped a little, but I still felt less of a man. "Coach, I was letting you fuck me like a girl."

"I fucked you like a man, goddamit!" The coach wasn't being mean. He wanted me to get it. I started to understand.

"It takes a real man to take another man's dick up his ass. Hell, I do it all the time. Am I a girl?"

I blushed. "No, sir."

"Damn right! I'm 100% man. I'm a coach. And if I want to fuck a handsome young man like you, or I want to take it in the ass from another man, I'm still a man. That never changes."

I felt better about it.

The coach smacked my bare ass, still wet with the dribble of come. "Now, pull up your shorts and shower up!"

3

MUSCLES AT THE BEACH

After that, me and the coach did a lot less sucking and a lot more fucking. After the first time, I didn't need him to stick his fingers in there. I just laid down on the bench and let him in. Sometimes he played with my titties, so I played back, which always made him come quicker. I loved pinching his big nipples, but I wanted it to last, so I held back as much as I could. When he played with my tits, I usually came. But I was younger, and I could come a bunch of times if I wanted. Sometimes I came three times. One afternoon, I came five times. The coach loved it. He said it made him feel really manly. Like he could fuck the come right out of me.

When it got warmer, that's when the bodybuilding competitions started. I wanted to please the coach in whatever way I could. Competing sounded scary. I had to get up on stage and let a bunch of people look at me. What if I was too little? What if my muscles were the wrong shape?

One Saturday, we drove out to Ocean Park in Santa Monica, and I saw Muscle Beach for the first time. All these guys were lifting weights and posing. When I walked up, every man turned and sized me up.

I heard a big black dude whistle. "Damn, son, you got a fine body."

I was hooked. I didn't realize how much I needed to feel like I belonged.

The black guy shook my hand. "I'm Billy Sunshine. Welcome to Muscle Beach." Several other guys came up and shook hands or clapped me on the back. This was where I belonged, and I knew it.

Billy Sunshine wore a tight swimsuit that didn't hide anything. His dick was wrapped around his hips to keep it from hanging out of the legs. When he squatted, his belly pressed against it. I tried not to look, but it was just so fucking huge.

He winked at me. "You ain't ready for it."

I felt the blood rush to my ears. He caught me looking. What did he mean "not ready for it?" Was he a fag, too?

Coach was right next to Billy. He said to him, "He's getting warmed up. But you're right. Maybe someone else before you." He pointed to Billy's crotch.

Right then, I knew what they were talking about, and it made me hard, not that anyone could tell. I was in baggy gym shorts and a cut-off t-shirt hanging down. Billy's nipples were bigger than my dick.

A big white dude with a German accent named Heimrich shook the coach's hand. "Ey, Hurley, you bring us some fresh meat?" He turned and looked at me through his squinty eyes. The gap between his teeth was the only thing wrong with his face. He was like the perfect man. Over six feet, and muscles that made mine look scrawny. He had big hands, big feet, big arms, big legs, and I figured everything else was big, too. He wore loose-fitting black shorts, so I couldn't see what was under them. Not like Billy and that fucking snake in his pants.

An older blond surfer dude named Kai showed me

around. He put an arm around my shoulders and squeezed. "Damn, dude, you're hella stacked."

I smiled. "Yeah, I work out."

"So do I, but I ain't got half of what you got."

I looked down and traced the outline of his cock in his shorts. He had way more than half of what I had. And he was soft. No telling how much bigger it really was! But I didn't say much. He followed my eyes down.

"I might have more down there. Most guys say so."

I was sorta weirded out by how much these guys talked about their bodies and dicks like it was no big deal. I had plenty of muscle and no dick. Kai was the opposite. I could see he worked out, but he was just skinny. He'd put on as much muscle as he could, but it wasn't much. That's when I realized why my dick didn't matter. Every guy wants what the other has if it's better. Kai wanted to be thick like me, and he wouldn't be. I wanted to be big like him, but that wasn't going to happen.

Kai spotted me while I did some bench presses. The guys gathered around to watch the new guy show off his jacked upper body. I did some barbell squats. Heimrich whistled as I pressed up from a squat.

"Mein Gott, that boy is blessed."

I knew he was talking about my ass. The other guys agreed. Lots of heads nodding, whispers. I knew the coach sure dug my ass. Maybe these guys would, too. That was putting it lightly, it turned out.

After push-ups, overhead presses, curls, and tricep lifts, I was jacked. My body was all shiny with sweat. I noticed there were bleachers where guys could watch. It was weird. A lot of guys were watching me, and it was a little creepy. They were fags, for sure. Not real men like my coach or the other bodybuilders. These were little prissy men who probably carried a purse when they went dancing. They were not real men like me. That's what I thought back then. I didn't know much about gay people or fags. I didn't think what me and coach did was fag shit because he was bisexual. I'd be bisexual, too, if my dick weren't so tiny. It's just the way I was built. At least, that's what I told myself. These guys were normal enough, but they wore sunglasses, so I couldn't tell where they were looking. By the way their mouths hung open, I figured they were looking right at my ass and thinking about how they wanted to fuck me. Fucking fags.

Heimrich brought me a towel to wipe off the sweat. He watched me the same way the coach always did. He was into my body. He was like a giant next to me. He scratched his balls quickly and adjusted. I still couldn't see what was under there. When he put a big hand on my shoulder, I felt his fingers touch my pec muscle. The palm was dry and warm.

"I wish I was short like you. Might you imagine how it would look, having these muscles on your body?" He vainly flexed a bicep. It was bigger than mine, yeah, but because he was tall, my muscles looked bigger. I flexed, and he smiled.

I said, "That's the way the cookie crumbles."

Heimrich made a face. "I don't understand."

His English wasn't as good as I thought. "Uh, yeah, I can't explain that. I think it means that we don't know how we're going to turn out because it isn't all up to us. Some people are big, some are small."

Heimrich looked down and smiled. "I got lucky, then." Again, he adjusted his crotch. This time, he squeezed it. It looked bigger than Coach's but nothing like Kai's or Billy's. "If you come back to my apartment, I show you." He pointed to a brick building down the beach toward Venice. "I live there."

Coach was a few feet away. He overheard and came over.

"So, Heimrich, you want to take him for a test drive? He can't flip. Too little."

I felt my dick get hard.

"Oh, that's too bad. This is how cookies crumble, eh?"

I laughed on the outside, but it hurt. I was pretty sure they were talking about my dick, and flipping meant that he took it up the ass, too. He was a few years older than me. His chest was perfectly smooth, not a hair in sight. He put on a pair of sandals and a tank top. He was so jacked that his nipples were outside the sleeves. I could do that. I just needed the right shirt. But I was thinking about all that because I was nervous. I'd only ever been with Coach Hurley. Heimrich was a lot bigger and more muscular than Coach. What would that be like? And he said he had a big dick. Was I ready for something bigger? Did I even want to do this?

Heimrich put his hand on my neck and guided me forward. It was a little humiliating.

I wriggled out of his grasp and turned to Coach like a dog someone was leaving at the pound.

"Will you still be here?"

Coach nodded. "Of course. This won't take long. Heimrich's fast."

❧ 4 ❧

DEUTSCH TREAT

Heimrich's place was tiny. It had no kitchen, just a hot plate, and a little square refrigerator. The bedroom was neat. His bed was tightly made.

He said, "Sit."

I sat on the bed. Heimrich stood over me. I looked up at his face. His smile with that gapped tooth made me feel warm. I realized he didn't have the windows open, and it was pretty damn hot in there.

"Can we open a window?"

"Sh!" he put a finger on my mouth. He took my hands and put them on his waistband. I pulled down. His dick was soft and didn't look much bigger than Coach Hurley's.

I chuckled. "You want me to suck it?"

He said, "Just so you get it hard, ja? Then we start the fucking."

I put the shriveled dick in my mouth and sucked on it. It swelled, stretching my lips.

THE DAMN THING INFLATED TO WAY MORE THAN twice its size, like a clown balloon. I would say it was about seven inches long and six inches around. He held the back of my head and pushed my tonsils until they hurt. Then he pushed past them! I'd never felt a dick in my throat before. I thought I might throw up, but I barely gagged. I guess the coach had really trained me well.

He said, "See, I told you my cookie crumbled." It made no sense, but I still knew what he meant. For the first time since I started sucking dick, I couldn't breathe through my nose, and I panicked. I pulled back and took a breath before he shoved me back down on it. Feeling it slide deep in my throat was so fucking hot. I hadn't realized you could even go there. Coach couldn't. He was too small. Heimrich's dick was stretching my jaw, too. It hurt a little, like a cramp. But I wanted to feel him in my throat, so I kept going down.

Then he pulled me off. "We fuck now." He spread a towel on the bed, but he shook his head when I asked if I should lie down.

He roughly pulled down my shorts and laughed. "Oh, Gott was unkind to you in front. He makes good in back, though."

He did something Coach had never done. He knelt down and buried his face in my butt. His big tongue lapped against my hole. I nearly jumped out of my skin. It felt great! I noticed a can of Crisco by his bedside. "Eew!" I thought. "Why would he eat Crisco in bed?"

He reached into the can and rubbed Crisco on his dick. He put the rest on my asshole and pressed against my hole. I was used to Coach Hurley, so I wasn't worried, even though maybe I should have been.

"You do this already before, ja?"

"Ja." I was making fun of him, but he didn't notice.

Then he just plowed into me. He was so much thicker than Coach. I saw stars again like I hadn't since that first day. I tried to pull off of him, but he held me still, waiting. After a minute, my ass adjusted. Then, in one glorious long stroke, he pushed to the end of my hole. He still had an inch or so to go.

"I warm you up then we go all the way."

I didn't know what the fuck that meant. Heimrich started fucking me hard, so his cock banged against the bottom of my hole, making me need to piss. It got worse.

"Dude, I gotta pee."

Without losing a beat, he grabbed a garbage can full of Kleenex beside his bed.

"Go there."

I felt a little humiliated as pee began leaking out of my tiny prick. Then it came in a stream. I held it so it pointed downward and only spilled a few drops. The more he banged into the back of my hole, the more pee trickled out until I was empty.

"Now we go all the way."

He lifted my left leg and pushed at an angle. I felt his dick slide to the left and then hit a spot that I never knew was in there. His thick dick was pressing the button down near the exit, but the tip of his dick was going through some kind of mystery hole. It didn't go far, just enough to make it feel extra good.

"This is better." He said it with the confidence of someone who had fucked a lot of guys. He knew it was better, and he was right. He picked up speed. With the Crisco, I didn't feel that friction I got with the thick, goopy Vaseline. It was a smooth ride. I made a note to buy the coach a can of this shit when we got back to LA.

With Coach Hurley, I had always felt like a son being taught by a father. Heimrich was more like a doctor with a patient. He was cold, even though the apartment was a steam bath. His movements were calculated and precise. They made him feel good, but I was left out. I felt good, yeah, but I didn't feel like he cared. He just figured I'd get what was coming to me, and that was enough.

I put my hand on my little nipple dick and played with it. Heimrich picked me up, twirled me around, and laid me face-up on the towel. He never missed a beat. His fucking was like an army drum, beating over and over with no change. He fucked like a robot. It felt good, especially because he was so deep up there, but I got bored. I played with his nipples.

"Ja! Squeeze them hard! Twist!"

I squeezed them, hoping it would speed things up. Heimrich pushed me away when I tried to kiss him. He held my mouth to his nipple. "Bite it! Hard!"

I chewed on it like a piece of old gum. It tasted like a young man, not the sweaty, hairy dad taste I was used to from Coach.

"I am close. Be prepared."

He acted like he was about to give me a shot at the doctor's office. Be prepared? What kind of fool says that?

I realized what he meant when he came so hard it squirted out of my ass onto the towel. With his fat cock, there was no extra room for his come. So it just shot out of me like a bullet.

I tried to come, but couldn't. Heimrich was the wrong man for me. I missed Coach. I liked his warm, furry belly. Heimrich was too smooth, too young, and too cold.

When it was over, he pulled me up by my armpits.

To my surprise, Hemirch said, "That was the best sex I ever had."

I didn't know how to answer back. "Oh, good." I didn't want a repeat. It wasn't bad, but it wasn't good enough. I liked Heimrich's cock. It was bigger than Coach's, but he didn't use it very well.

We walked back to Muscle Beach, where the bodybuilders made catcalls. I was tired of being embarrassed, so I just decided not to be.

Coach took me aside. "How was it?"

I shrugged. "Okay. He's bigger. You're better."

The coach laughed and slapped me on the back. "Let's go home. I'll fuck you right."

❦   5   ❦

TEA ROOM

The following Saturday was hot as hell. I mean that in more than one way. Coach drove me to the beach. On the way there, he stopped at Lafayette Park.

"What are we doing here?"

Coach smiled. "Come on, let me show you something new."

I was out of holes, so I couldn't imagine what he would show me next. But he didn't mean a new way to fuck. He was talking about cruising, something I barely knew about.

We headed for the restroom. "They call this a Tea Room. When you get inside, don't say anything. There's a code of silence."

I was pretty confused until we walked into a fucking orgy. The men's room was a fucking sucking room full of fags. There were businessmen, bums, Blacks, Whites, Mexicans, every type of guy you've ever met, and then some you didn't know about.

A bunch of hands came at me. An Oriental grabbed my crotch and then stepped back, scampering off. It wasn't a very good start. But then a big guy, maybe Mexican, maybe White, put his hands on my shoulders and nodded to an empty stall. He had dark red hair and freckles and wore tight blue jeans with a white cowboy hat. He was the whitest Mexican I ever seen. He whispered something that sounded like "Seeyentatay" and pushed me down on the toilet seat. He unzipped his pants and pulled out the hugest fucking freckled dick. His pubes matched his hair. I opened wide, thinking maybe this wouldn't work, but he didn't wait. He grabbed both ears and pulled me close, shoving that meat stick down my throat. I was lucky I'd practiced a little with Heimrich. His thing went way deeper and stretched my throat so bad it hurt. My lips were spread as far as they could go and then a little more. I felt the corners cracking a little.

He said, "See Poppy." He reached through the sleeve of my tank top and rubbed my chest. His hands were rough, like someone who did a lot of hard labor. It felt good the way his callouses bumped across my titties.

He held my head and fucked my mouth like a pussy. I can't explain it, but he tasted like he had a lot of kids. I know, it's weird. But he was a fertile man. The way his big dick slipped down my throat felt so good I got light-headed. I let him stay in my throat way too long, and I got even dizzier. Just before I passed out, he pulled out. I let out my breath real loud, and someone shushed us. I started laughing, but the cowboy didn't think it was funny. He smacked my face and stuck his dick down my throat again. I didn't gag once. I was in control of my body, all of it. I think most guys are up in their heads too much. I was way down in my body and loving this. I thought he would stop and turn me around like Coach always did, but when I tried to stand up, he pushed me back down hard, never letting his cock fall out of my mouth. I guess he didn't like fucking. I put my hand in my gym trunks and played with myself. I didn't want to come, because it would show when I got to the beach.

Outside the stall, I saw Coach bent over a sink

taking it up the ass from a Black dude. I knew he was in pain because I could hear him. I felt sad for a split second, thinking how I could never make him feel like that. But that king-sized cock in my throat was leaking, and I had to pay attention.

Then something new happened. My throat started to squeeze the guy's dick on its own. He looked down at me with a huge grin. I could hear his breath whistling through his teeth. I wasn't doing it, not with my mind, anyway. It did the trick. He came so far down my throat that I didn't have a choice but to swallow. I felt warm juice head towards my stomach.

He pulled out and walked out of the bathroom without so much as a thank you. Another man stepped into the booth, but my throat was sore. I could hear the black dude getting ready to come with Coach, who was almost crying.

I had to see what was making him hurt. I stepped up to the sink. The Black guy gave me a big white-toothed grin and whispered. "This your daddy?"

I shook my head.

"He's about to get some."

I saw the thickest dick I'd ever imagined. He was deep, and I didn't know how long it was, but it would have made me cry, too. The black guy's breath changed that way a guy does when he's gonna come. He held himself all the way inside Coach, and I could see his big black balls pumping. He stayed there a while. When he pulled out, I was amazed. Inch after inch just kept coming out of Coach's ass. Like a dead snake, the fucking thing popped out and slapped the black guy's thigh so loud it clapped. Coach's hole was a big 'O'. Come came out and fell on the tiles. I noticed the floor for the first time. There was come everywhere. A man could slip and break his neck if he wasn't careful.

"Come on." Coach grabbed my arm, and we left the

bathroom. He could barely walk, so he put one arm over my shoulder.

"That thing was fucking huge," I said. My throat was sore. It came out like a frog.

Coach talked like he was lifting weights and out of breath. "Yeah, son, I bit off more than I could chew with that one.

❧ 6 ❧

SURF'S UP

When we got to the beach, Coach was still limping. I could hear the guys talking about it. They weren't mean, but they laughed a lot. Coach looked embarrassed.

"Hey, Shamus. What's kickin'?" It was Kai

"Hey, bud," I croaked.

Kai laughed. "Coach got fucked, and you must have sucked some major dick!"

Now, it was my turn to be embarrassed. "Yeah."

"Cool. Maybe later you can suck mine."

I doubted it. I'd seen what Kai had, at least the outline. My throat was so raw I didn't think I should try again with him.

Coach didn't even try to spot me, let alone lift weights. Kai was my spotter. The men were impressed. I wasn't the strongest, but my body was awesome. Guys commented on how my lats were so wide and my tits were so big. I'd done a lot with my quads, too. When I worked them, I heard more than one guy say, "Look at that ass!"

I knew those guys all wanted to fuck me. I was proud of it. I think it was then that sex moved into first place over bodybuilding. Well, it was a tie. My ass quivered thinking about a big dick up there. Hell, I'd take a little one if I had to. I just needed to get fucked. Maybe Kai would fuck me.

While I pressed, Kai stood so I could see he didn't have no underwear under his long board shorts. His dick was soft, but it hung halfway to his knee.

I said, "Kai, my throat is wrecked. But you can fuck me if you want."

Kai stepped back. "Dude, I ain't no fag."

That was confusing. He'd just said I could suck his dick.

"You don't wanna fuck me?"

Kai smiled. "I didn't say that. You took me by surprise, brah."

I finished my set. My little dick was rock hard, but nobody could tell. I kept thinking about that big blond surfer dick in board shorts. Soft, it looked almost as long as Heimrich's hard. It was skinny, though.

I turned to Coach. "I'm gonna hang out with Kai for a bit."

Coach checked his watch. "Okay, be back in two hours. I'm going over there." He nodded towards the changing rooms. I watched him limp over there. I wondered if the same stuff happened there, too. It did.

Kai's place was the opposite of Heimrich's. It was a one-bedroom with lots of space. He wasn't right on the beach. The whole apartment was a pigsty. I don't think he cleaned except maybe to throw away the garbage. Piles of dirty clothes were everywhere. He swept a few piles off his bed.

"I go deep. Especially a short guy like you. You clean?"

I had never been asked that before. He pointed to the bathroom. "Go take a shit. Come back naked."

He said it so casual I didn't get mad. It just felt natural, like he asked everybody to take a dump first. With Coach, I hadn't even thought about it. How deep did he mean? I thought about that spot that Heimrich kept pressing. Did Kai go inside there? Yes. Yes, he did, it turns out.

I took a shit and came out naked. Kai put his finger in a jar of coconut oil.

"Come here. Bend over." I liked how he was bossy. He was older than Heimrich, and he had a hairy chest. I guessed he was maybe thirty years old. He was skinny, but all that weightlifting made every muscle stand out. His stomach had eight abs!

I bent over and spread my cheeks. Kai put a long, thin finger up my ass and swirled it around. He pulled it out, inspecting it.

"Hot damn! You're clean. Let's go."

Kai stripped. His soft cock was swelling. It mostly got longer. As it stood up off his legs, I was surprised. I could see his heartbeat in that thing the way it pulsed. The shaft was thin, but the head was pretty fat in comparison.

I got on all fours on his bed.

He said, "Dude, you are so fucking beautiful."

Kai's arms weren't quite long enough to reach my waist when he aimed the tip at my hole. I felt him slide between my rock-hard ass muscles and push easily through my hole. Then he grabbed my waist. He pushed steady until he bumped the back, and then he turned left. But he didn't stop like Heimrich. He kept going. I saw stars when his mushroom head snapped past that hole. But it didn't last. He pushed two or three more inches into my guts before his hips smacked into my big, round ass. He held the cheeks apart and pushed in another half inch.

When he pulled back, popping through that hole, it felt like I was taking the best shit of my life. He dragged the head so it was right about to pop out of my asshole, and when he did, it pressed that button.

Slowly, Kai pushed it in and dragged it out. It didn't matter if he was coming or going; it felt fucking fantastic. I liked how easy it was, being thin and all. Each time his dick popped past that second hole, I heard a clapping sound.

Kai said, "Dude, your ass is perfect!"

My throat was still sore, so when I said, "Thanks," it sounded like I'd said, "Eggs."

When he knew he had a straight shot, he picked up the pace. In long strokes, he pulled and pushed like a piston in a chamber. The clapping sound got faster, like one person applauding at a speech. I squeezed my ass to grip him better.

"Yeah, Shamus, hold it like that."

I squeezed and gripped the shaft with my hole. I held it like that the whole time, feeling Kai's dick rub against me. It was so hot.

Kai kept going deep. I spread my ass cheeks wide so he could slide all the way in. Each time he passed that inner hole, I felt something building. Not like the way you're gonna shoot a load. It was different. My stomach tingled. On all fours, facing down, my guts tightened and let go. Then they did it again, just like my throat with that cowboy.

"Holy shit! Dude, you're coming like a girl."

Kai was right. I didn't care if he called me a girl because it felt so fucking good. I tried to hold still, but my ass and hips kept twitching, and my guts kept squeezing Kai's skinny cock as he plunged in faster and harder.

I said, "I gotta lay down, or I'm gonna fall."

With his dick jammed deep up my ass, I rolled onto my back and wrapped my strong legs around his waist. I could just see his white butt fly up into the air, and his brown waist, tanned from weeks of surfing and lifting. I couldn't hold him all the way, so I let his ass slip past my fingers at the top, then grabbed on the way down, pulling his cock inside me until his pubes brushed my balls.

I couldn't help but look him in the eyes. He stared back, smiling.

"Don't get no ideas, dude. I'm straight."

I looked away. That hurt, but not bad. It made me feel stupid.

I held my ankles, so my ass went higher. Kai put his hands on either side of my head like he was doing a plank and pounded me so hard my guts started up again. This time, on my back, it felt even better. I didn't care if it made my legs and arms weak because I didn't need them. I was right where Kai needed me. Gravity did all the work. And that twitch and squeeze was none of my doing.

I saw that look on Kai's face and heard his breaths get shorter. All of his muscles stood out. I put a hand on his furry chest and brushed a nipple. That was all he needed.

"Oh, dude, I'm gonna fuckin' come. I'm coming! I'm...Aargh!"

As he said it, he pushed all the way inside me. My body was still shaking and squeezing him. It felt like I was milking a cow way up inside me. His come went so deep that I probably wouldn't see it until the next time I took a shit. My belly felt warm.

He fell on top of me, his furry chest rubbing against my smooth body. I watched the ceiling fan spin, tripping on how it sometimes looked like it was spinning in the opposite direction. I wanted to kiss Kai. I lifted my head, but he turned away.

He said, "Dude, I said I was straight."

BILLY'S PLACE

We were at the end of the term. I was going to graduate soon. I had no plans to go to college. I studied for the SATs, but all I learned was a few big words and some compound sentences, but not much else. I got low scores. Coach suggested I go to Santa Monica Community College because they teach weightlifting. Not that I needed a teacher, but I needed somewhere to work out besides Muscle Beach. I got in on probation. They said I had to take Math over the summer. I fucking hate Math, but it was okay.

The college had a housing office where I found a bachelor apartment in the same building as Heimrich, right on the beach. The college was just a short bike ride up Pico. It was perfect. I could work out the whole day. Ride my bike to summer school, work out, ride my bike to the beach, work out. I wanted to be a champion.

Speaking of champions, I signed up for the Mister Muscle Beach contest in July. In June, I graduated from Belmont High with no honors. The coach said it didn't matter. I wasn't the kind of guy to go off to some fancy school. I belonged with the bodybuilders for now. He gave me a big hug and took me up to his office. That was one of the last times we fucked.

I didn't make any money, but the school gave me a job to pay the 30 bucks a month for rent, with money left over for food. I worked in the college locker room, handing out towels. It was like being a kid in a candy store. I loved big dicks, and there were a few. Summer was slow at the college, but I saw some big swingers. I wore sunglasses while I worked and told anyone who asked that I was sensitive to light. I took a few guys home and let them fuck me. They were just kids, really, like me. It wasn't as hot as when I was with someone older.

Oh, and I didn't tell you about me and Billy Sunshine. Yeah, you guessed it, though. We fucked. I didn't think I would ever take another dick like his, not anywhere. My first week after graduation, he came up to me in the changing area and said, "I don't know if you could take it. Do you wanna try?"

His cock was wrapped up around his hips so far, it almost touched his back. It was throbbing through his tight swimsuit, too. We were alone, so I touched his giant dick. It felt softer than the other dicks I'd tried. My hand only reached halfway around. It was like three beer cans wrapped in foam. He lifted part of it out from the middle. It was dark and veiny.

"Yeah, I could try."

"You sure, baby?"

I didn't think I'd like being called baby, but coming from Billy Sunshine, it felt good. "Yeah."

After our workout, we went to his house in Venice. He lived on one of the canals. It was nice going to a house for a change. Billy had a record player. He put on some jazz and poured me a glass of wine. I didn't drink much, so the wine went to my head pretty fast.

Billy said, "I gotta kiss to get in the mood. You like kissing?"

I said, "I ain't no fag, but yeah, I'll kiss you."

Billy was the best kisser I ever knew. He sucked on my lips and blew air in my mouth so we could keep kissing. His hands were everywhere, rubbing my nipples, my ass, my little dick, my thighs, and places I didn't even know felt good, like between my balls and my ass. He picked me up like a little kid, holding my ass against his crotch, lifting me up and down so I rubbed on his dick.

Billy carried me to the bathroom. He filled a hot water bottle and said, "Do you know what this is?" He held up a long white hose.

I shook my head.

He spat in his hand and put a slippery finger just inside my hole. Then he shoved that hose right up my ass.

"Tell me when it starts to hurt." He opened a clamp, and water filled my guts.

"Okay, now."

Billy squeezed the clamp shut. "Hold it, baby." He pulled the hose out of my ass. I needed to go real bad. He set me down on the toilet and closed the door. I shit like I'd never shit before. When I flushed, Billy came back.

"We gotta do it again, baby."

This time it was mostly water and just a little bit of leftover shit. Billy checked the toilet before I flushed.

"Let's do it." He picked me up and carried me upstairs to his bedroom. It was dark. It smelled like incense and sweat. He turned on a dim lamp as he undressed.

He took off his sweatshirt. His chest was broad and shiny. His nipples were dark against his black skin. He lifted me to my feet and held my mouth to his chest. I sucked on his nipples like a baby.

"Mmm, yeah." He held me there while I nursed. I

could feel his big dick lifting off his leg, bumping into my thigh. I squeezed it.

"Ooh, yeah, baby. Just like that."

His lips were big and squishy, like his dick. He tasted like wine. He lifted me and set me on his bed. I watched him take off his sweats. His cock had fallen out of his swimsuit and hung hard away from his legs. His balls were still in the swimsuit. He pulled it down. They fell out. They were huge, like two tennis balls in a bag.

He held his cock up. It was so heavy that it sagged a little. He slicked it up with Vaseline while he watched me undress. I was embarrassed by how small my dick was. His was honestly 100 times bigger. I mean, I didn't do the math, but it was probably close.

"Yeah, baby, you got a little clit down there."

I should have been mad. I wasn't. I felt good because Billy liked it.

He said, "Go ahead, rub that little thing. Get it hard."

I blushed. "It already is."

Billy sucked air between his teeth. "Fuck, that's hot." He knelt and put his big mouth on my little dick, licking and sucking it. He used his tongue to tease and flick it back and forth. It felt good. I moaned.

Billy pinched my titties while he sucked me. I felt that familiar rush right before coming.

"Billy, I'm gonna come."

"Mmmhmm." He kept sucking until I couldn't wait anymore. I blew a load in his mouth. He lapped it up, cleaning my cock with his tongue.

"Ooh, you white boys taste good. You ready?"

I nodded.

He stayed on his knees and put his dick head against my asshole. It was so fucking long that he didn't need to stand up! I knew it was gonna hurt. But it surprised me. He was hard, but his dick was spongy. It slipped in, stretching my hole, but it didn't tear me in two like it looked. I felt it wriggle in me like a snake. He stood up. His cock turned the corner and just kept going. He was longer than Kai. He was so thick that I could see the outline of his cock on my belly. I rubbed it, fascinated.

He said, "Yeah, rub it like that. Right through your skin."

I pressed and rubbed against my belly, feeling the cock slide inside farther until his hips hit my butt. It was deeper than any of the guys had ever gone. He stayed in there, just tugging and pushing. He didn't take long strokes like Kai. He had this rhythm all his own. Fast-Fast, Slow. Slow. Fast. Slow. I was in heaven.

He picked me up and carried me downstairs to the couch, where the jazz record was playing. I realized where he got that rhythm. He fucked in time to the music.

Then he said, "You ready?"

"Ready for what?"

Billy grinned. "I'm gonna cut loose on your ass."

And he did. He fucked me so hard I thought I would pass out. He was fast. I couldn't help myself. I cried like a girl, but he didn't stop, and I didn't want him to. I just wailed. It got louder as he went in and quieter as he pulled out. Oh man, it was good.

"You like that, white boy?"

"Fuck yeah."

He tipped me up so my legs were in the sky. He fucked downward. At one point, he lost his grip, and he musta thought I was gonna fall. But he didn't know I was a gymnast. I stood steady on my hands, upside down, while he fucked me harder and harder. I lowered my knees to my chest, still in a headstand, then brought them up and hitched them around his waist.

"Boy, you some kinda acrobat?"

I didn't answer. I did a sit-up so I was upright with

my ass hanging off the back of the couch. He never stopped fucking me. I grabbed hold of his shoulders and lifted myself up. He carried me to the kitchen and fucked me on the table. I never had this much fun during sex. Billy was amazing.

Back upstairs on Billy's bed, I lay on my side, and he fucked me from behind. I felt that little twitch in my gut that meant I was about to come like a woman again. It happened a second time, then a third, and then I pulsed fast.

"Oh shit, boy, you doing something crazy to my dick. Damn, that's good!"

I stayed on my side, relaxed, letting Billy fuck the shit out of me while my guts twisted and squeezed him back. I might have passed out a little. It just felt too good.

The next thing I remember, he said, "Get ready, boy. I'm about to come."

I rubbed my dick between my thumb and finger. Billy held me by the neck, choking me lightly, holding on so he could fuck harder and faster. My insides were so stretched out, but they just kept squeezing and pushing against Billy's cock. I watched it move against my belly. When I pressed down, he came.

"Ohhhhh! Yeah! Yeah!" He was so into it. As I felt the warm gyzym flow up inside me, I went over the edge and shot a load on his sheets.

I thought it was over, but he started that jazzy rhythm again, fucking fast and slow.

"It ain't over, baby. Billy Sunshine fucks all night. You in?"

"Yeah."

It lasted until we fell asleep in the middle of the night, his dick still up inside me. When I woke up the next morning, he was downstairs in the kitchen.

I limped downstairs. My ass hurt, but it felt good,

like after a heavy workout. We were both naked in the kitchen.

"I made you breakfast, baby." He spooned some eggs on my plate and topped it with a fat sausage. I laughed.

I said, "That reminds me of you."

He winked. "It's a lot smaller, baby, a lot smaller."

WINNING BIG ISN'T
EVERYTHING

The Santa Monica City Council was giving all of us a lot of shit. They thought us bodybuilders were a big nuisance, just cluttering up the boardwalk and engaging in "perverted activities," as they called it. Yeah, well fuck 'em.

I worked out twice a day, getting ready for that Mr. Muscle Beach contest. My ass got rounder, my legs and arms were like tree trunks. Well, short tree trunks, but you get the picture. My chest was as big around as Lana Turner's. I was at my peak. Heimrich taught me how to eat right. I had a lot of chicken breast fried up in no oil on my hot plate. I ate green vegetables and rice cooked with egg whites. I had to throw away the yolks. He tried to convince me to have raw egg whites every morning, but it made me gag. It was too much like swallowing ten loads of gyzym. I couldn't hack it.

When I worked out at the beach, I always took notice of the guys walking by. I don't know why, but it was the ones who didn't even look at me that got me the hottest. The Ocean Park Pier was home to the Z-Boys, a bunch of renegade surfers who risked their lives surfing by the pier. There was one Z-Boy from the Valley that Kai knew. One day, he walked right past us, nose in the air, heading for the waves. I saw something bizarre. It looked like he had a rolled-up towel tucked so far under his legs that it stuck in his butt cheeks. I asked Kai about him.

"Oh, that's Rocco Pounder. Nice dude. He's super embarrassed of his weiner, though. It makes Billy Sunshine's dick look like a Vienna sausage."

I studied his weird walk and realized he had the thing tucked between his legs and crawling up his back. He bent to take off his shoes, and I swear I saw that fat cock head poking out of the waist of his shorts! Fuck, that was hot. But he didn't even know I existed.

Kai said, "Forget it, dude. I heard he put a honey in the hospital."

That was hot. I wanted to see Rocco Pounder fuck a girl. Or maybe I just wanted him to fuck me. But I was invisible.

I liked the guys who didn't see me. It was weird. If they weren't a bodybuilder, I didn't want them unless they wanted nothing to do with me. Those perverts in the bleachers watching me work out just pissed me off. Fuck, guys, look at Kai! He may not have that body, but he still lifts. Get off your asses and stop looking at me! It makes me nervous.

The night of the competition, my attitude changed a little. I felt too much at the same time. I was scared to get on stage. I was embarrassed how small my dick was in the little swimsuit. I was proud of my hard work. I wanted to win, but I didn't want to risk losing. When they called my name, I didn't move.

"Get out there, son!"

I whirled around. It was Coach. He was there! He pushed me, so I had no choice. I stepped out on that stage and flexed. When everybody out in the audience cheered, I loved it. I didn't care if it was a bunch of fags and their girlfriends. I knew right then that I found my place on this earth. I was a competitive bodybuilder. Period. When I looked around at the other guys com-

peting, I noticed a lot of them didn't have much between their legs. Guys like Kai, Heimrich, or Billy were
the exceptions. To tell the truth, most of these guys
looked like me down there. And it made their legs look
bigger, just like Coach had told me.

One thing I was sure of. When the judges had us
turn around to flex from the back, I heard a lot of whis-
tles. I knew, without even looking, that they were
whistling at me. I had the best ass, period. Too bad it
wasn't just an ass contest. They kept eliminating guys
until it was just me and Heimrich. He was technically
perfect, and I can't deny it. His ass was boring, but his
body was tall and perfect. Still, I won second prize that
night. When the audience cheered for me, it was the
best feeling in the world. And I was determined to beat
that fucker the next time.

I invited Coach and the guys back to my little apartment. We stopped and got a bottle of Jim Beam on the
way. A couple of Jim and Cokes later, I was in a pretty
good mood. I had to lay off everything for the last six
weeks, and it was time to cut loose.

Kai and Billy weren't in the contest, so I asked them
why not.

Kai said, "Dude, look at me. I'm as fit as any of you,
but it doesn't look the way they want. I ain't no Steve
Reeves."

Billy laughed. "I ain't neither. Look at me. But that
ain't why I don't compete. I lift weights so I can be the
biggest, baddest black motherfucker in town. I don't
give a shit about ribbons."

I lifted the ribbon on my chest and frowned.

Billy said, "No, I don't mean it like that, Shamus.
You should be mighty proud for a first-timer."

I said, "Oh, cool."

Billy said, "Nah, I mean, I don't need someone else
to tell me I'm good anymore. Sometimes, those judges
were prejudiced, and I knew I should win, but I didn't.

I let it get to me. Then I realized it don't mean shit. All that mattered was me."

Coach said, "And here I thought it was because you couldn't fit that fucking thing in your posing strap!"

Billy laughed, grabbed Coach Hurley, and pinned him on my bed. "You're gonna take that back!"

Coach said, "I'll take it wherever you wanna put it."

Kai and Heimrich whistled. "Do it, Billy!"

We were all a little drunk. I stood up and stripped, kneeling on my bed. I sucked my coach, my first lover, while Billy invaded his asshole. Kai put his tongue in my ass, and Heimrich stuck his fat cock in Coach's mouth. We were a sex machine. For hours, we just kept finding new ways to fuck or be fucked. I missed Coach. I wanted to be alone with him, but I shared him just like the others shared me. I remember a moment when I was on my back, my legs wrapped around Coach, kissing him while he fucked me hard. Kai was behind him, fucking him at the same time. Even though he wasn't big and didn't go deep, that moment we were together turned on that pulsing in my ass. I squeezed his cock and made him come in under a minute. When he pulled out, I knew it was goodbye. Heimrich and Kai stuck both their dicks in me at the same time while I watched Coach walk out of my apartment for the first and last time. I was alone in my bed when the night turned into day.

After the competition, I started checking out my fans in the bleachers, just casually, not cruising or nothing. I stopped thinking of them as just queers. I liked the attention more. I still thought they were fags, though. Was I a fag? No, because I was a bodybuilder, and there's a difference!

There was this one guy who was so fucking big, I could see it from fifty feet away. He watched me like a buzzard sitting on a dying horse. Except he was the horse. I eventually found out what he wanted from me. And I was all too happy to give it to him.

[Editor's note: Shamus's autobiography leaves off here. The rest of his story reads more like fiction. Enjoy!]

SHAMUS SHORTS

MUSCLE BEACH

Taryn Rearden was a muscle fan. He didn't have the right frame for it, but he loved watching strong men lift weights. His favorite pastime on a Saturday afternoon was watching the bodybuilders at Muscle Beach in Santa Monica. He would grab a hot dog on a stick and a lemonade, find a good spot in the bleachers, and stare at the sea of men devoted to their physique.

One muscleman, Shamus Little, had caught Taryn's eye. Watching Shamus squat, clean, and jerk, Taryn would put a hand near his knee and furtively play with the tip of his huge penis. Shamus had been gifted with a remarkable pair of teardrop-shaped buttocks. The muscles would contract when he squatted, forming a tight valentine in his posing strap. He could crack walnuts. Shamus rarely looked out towards the bleachers. He was committed to self-improvement. No amount of self-improvement would ever fix the Irish curse. Shamus had a magnificent backside and an incredible body, but he was all balls and no dick in the front. Taryn wasn't interested in Shamus for his dick. It was that ass, his chunky thighs, and his rippling torso that made Taryn so hot for him. Shamus had a salesman's smile to complement his handsome face. His square jaw and brown eyes could melt the heart of an enraged bull. His long lashes only made his beauty stand out atop the muscular frame.

Taryn was lost in a daydream, staring glassy-eyed at that perfect Irish ass, when he heard a shout.

"Hey! Hey faggot! What the fuck you lookin' at"? It was Shamus. Taryn pointed to himself.

"Yes, you, you fucking fag!"

Taryn hated that word. Hearing something so ugly erupt from the mouth of such an angelic man only made it worse.

"Come here!" Shamus commanded. Taryn obeyed.

"Is that thing for real"? Shamus pointed to the semi-hard cock snaking down Taryn's left pant leg.

"Yeah, it's real."

"I ain't no fag, but I wanna see it, yeah"?

Taryn looked down at his monster and smiled. Shamus smiled back, and he nearly melted.

Shamus Little lived in a bachelor apartment on Speedway. The interior hadn't been painted since before the war. Shamus wasn't a slob, but he wasn't tidy, either. His sink was full of dishes. His bathroom didn't smell too pretty. But his laundry was folded, and his garbage was taken out.

"Yeah, uh, sorry about the mess. I eat a lot of eggs in the morning."

Taryn shrugged.

"Hey, uh, I gotta use the crapper. Have a seat." Shamus patted his unmade bed.

"Should I get naked for you"?

"No! Wait for me."

As Shamus closed the door, Taryn saw him grab a rubber enema bag hanging in the shower. Soon the explosive sounds of forcibly expelled water and shit came from the bathroom. After a pause, a second round of water gushed into the toilet in a steady stream.

Shamus emerged.

"Yeah, all that protein gets clogged when I lift. Sometimes, I need a little help to get it moving."

Taryn knew he did it for another reason. Thinking about it gave him half a hard-on. Shamus stared in fascination as the summer sausage became a salami. His little dick was growing hard in his posing strap.

"Listen, Shamus, if I don't get these pants off now, my dick will get trapped.

"Oh, damn, that is the hottest fucking problem! Go ahead."

I struggled to release my cock from its cloth prison. Shamus helped pull the jeans to my ankles. He was rewarded with a hard flesh uppercut to his square jaw.

"Holy shit, dude! That fucker is unreal."

"Oh, it's real."

"You fuck a lot of chicks with it"? Shamus had his hand in his bikini, rolling his little penis between two fingers.

"Women aren't built to handle it."

"You can't fuck women"?

"I could do serious damage."

Shamus shook his head in amazement. "Damn, dude. So what, you fuck guys"?

"They're too afraid."

"Afraid of a little pain"?

"It's more than a little."

"Bullshit. I'll bet you I could handle it." He shook his ass cheeks. "I ain't afraid of a little pain."

"Prove it."

Shamus pulled a can of Crisco from the cupboard.

Taryn sighed as Shamus spread shortening along the vast meaty cock. He was growing to full size now. He wondered if Shamus had second thoughts.

Taryn's cock swelled even further when Shamus inserted several slick fingers into that perfect ass. He stretched his hole using three fingers. It was just like a bodybuilder to do warm-up exercises before getting fucked.

Shamus issued a disclaimer. "Remember, this is a bet. I am not a fag."

"Sure you're not," Taryn thought as he stepped towards his target.

This was not the bleachers. Taryn had a close-up view of his obsession, Shamus, and his bulbous ass. The muscleman bent forward and separated his tear-shaped buttocks for Taryn, exposing a greasy pink hole buried in soft mounds of ass.

Taryn prepared himself for disappointment. He had been this far with many men, but most screamed and gave up; in his lifetime, only two men lasted until the end.

He pushed his baseball-sized cockhead against the twitching pink hole.

"Are you ready"?

"Do it quick, man."

Taryn leaned into the bodybuilder. His cock penetrated the slippery ring and traveled rapidly to the end of Shamus's rectum. There were several inches to go but nowhere to put them.

Shamus sucked air between his teeth, then blew it out in measured bursts. His huge back ran with sweat. His tiny waist wriggled in discomfort, which gave Taryn an unexpected thrill.

"Keep going," Shamus said.

Taryn was puzzled. He had reached the end. This was as far as he could go.

"That's it, man. No more room."

Shamus looked over his shoulder. "Past the second sphincter, dude."

Taryn didn't know what to do. Shamus sighed, twisting to the left. "Here"!

And like magic, his cock found another hole deep

inside Shamus. He pressed against it, but it was tight. Shamus pounded the mattress. "Smack my ass!"

Taryn thought about the name-calling earlier and used that as fuel to strike the bodybuilder's butt cheek with a resounding crack. Shamus gave an astonished gasp.

The hole loosened. Taryn entered the inner chamber. He never knew it was there. His hips slid forward, resting against the massive globes of butt muscle he had admired for so many months.

Between grunts and moans, Shamus said, "Deeper!" He pulled his butt cheeks far apart so Taryn's pubic mound pressed hard against the bodybuilder's soft, greasy anus.

Taryn had never gone deeper than 7 inches. Now, he was fully engulfed in Shamus's sausage casing; it was ecstasy.

Shamus spoke through his pain. "See. I told you aaah I could take it...ow...Now that...ay! Now that you're in, you ooooh might as well fu-u-uck me!"

Taryn ground his hips against the luscious buttocks. He wanted to stay inside.

"Harder, longer, faster! I can take it."

Taryn pulled and then thrust his hips, slipping in and out of the deep rectum. He ignored the bodybuilder's cries of pain. He focused only on his cock. He felt Shamus jerking his little dick. He wanted to help. He reached under and cupped the man's giant balls.

"Hey man, your balls are bigger than mine!"

"For real"? Shamus was smiling.

They were. Taryn's enormous cock had only normal-sized balls. They were dwarfed when he was fully hard. Shamus reached back until he found them. He laughed.

"You got me beat in the dick department, but I got a better body and bigger balls."

Taryn felt a moment's pity for this insecure man. It

is fucking hard to carry around an enormous penis. It must be rough to live with a tiny one, too.

Shamus ground his ass-backward into Taryn's hips, then pulled away. There was so much dick they could both fuck back and forth without fear of the gigantic cock falling out.

Like an acrobat, Shamus used his powerful arms to pivot through space, landing on his back in missionary, Taryn's cock still firmly lodged in his muscular ass. Shamus squeezed his outer sphincter to massage the base of the monstrous dick. The man's muscles were all strong, including the sphincter. He milked Taryn like a Guernsey cow.

Taryn put Shamus's hamstrings against his chest; the bodybuilder's lower legs dangled over his shoulders. This position gave him leverage to cut loose and pound the snot out of Shamus.

Indeed, like a runny nose, Shamus began to leak from his little cock head.

"Oh, fuck yeah. Oh fuck! You're making my ass into a pussy. See my clit dripping"?

Taryn liked this role-playing. "Your pussy is gonna be so loose when I'm done with you"!

Shamus placed one of Taryn's hands on a tiny brown nipple, gracing his massive chest muscle. "You like my tits"?

"Your tits are so big, like your huge fucking ass."

"Play with my tiny clit."

Taryn jerked Shamus's tiny penis with two fingers. The muscleman leaned his head back and moaned like a woman."

"Oh fuck! You're fucking my pussy too hard! I'm gonna split open"!

Taryn's two fingers were getting wet. He held them to his nose, then licked them. "Your pussy juice tastes good."

"Does it? Oh, I want a taste. Give me some."

Taryn scooped up a generous helping of clear seminal fluid and fed it to the hungry bodybuilder.

"Oh, I'm gonna come for real! Watch out."

Entirely on its own, no hands, Shamus's little cock shot right into Taryn's face. For such a small barrel, his gun had a lot of bullets and a long range. Those bouncing balls created a mess on Taryn's face, neck, and chest. The muscleman lay back and surveyed his handiwork.

"I got you good." He grinned, and butter melted somewhere.

"Shamus, you finished. Do you want me to stop"?

"Hell no! Look!" He pointed to his rock-hard cock, "That was just the first batch. I can make a gallon of the shit if you fuck me long enough."

"Yeah, this guy isn't a faggot," Taryn mused in silence.

The tricks didn't stop there. Shamus twirled into a headstand, his legs split in a wide V. Taryn fucked down into his hole like an oil derrick.

In another pose, Shamus was so limber that he could do the splits across Taryn's lap, then bounce using only his groin muscles for leverage.

Because of Taryn's incredible length, in one position, he could put his tongue in the hole and taste it when Shamus rode the top five inches. Shamus started dripping again, howling with delight.

He rotated and sat down hard, facing Taryn, completely filled with cock. He tipped his head and grazed Taryn's mouth with his jawbone. Taryn grabbed his head and kissed so hard he licked his tonsils.

Shamus pulled away. "Man, I don't kiss. But if you need to so you can come, then-"

"Shut up." They locked lips and embraced. Shamus used his thigh muscles to squat and lift, rubbing his insides hard with the big dick. Taryn had never kissed someone while fucking. He didn't realize until it was too late; the kiss put him over the edge.

Shamus could sense it coming. With more acrobatics, he ended on all fours, giving Taryn complete control over the strokes. Taryn cradled the tiny dick and enormous balls as he took his last, long strokes.

"Oh fuck! I'm gonna come!"

"Come in my pussy!"

"Your pussy better be ready for this." Taryn got very hot in his ball sac. A pulse began at the base of his cock, and took the long journey to the tip. This repeated; each time, the pulse grew more urgent.

Shamus took back his balls and pounded his itty bitty dick. He could come on command. He jacked in a holding pattern, waiting for Taryn's sperm to enter him.

The urgent pulse became an electrical vibration. Taryn's legs shook.

"Fuck! Oh fuck Shamus! Oh shit! I'm coming"!

A molten hot flow of white lava spurted out of Taryn, basting Shamus with melted man butter. At the first eruption, Taryn was all the way inside Shamus. It coated his left colon. He pulled into the rectum for the remaining squirts. It filled and shot out the sides of the muscle man's rectum. For the first time since he penetrated Shamus, he allowed his cock to slip out.

Along with it came a sea of buttery sperm. Shamus's gash was wide open, curved, and perfectly round, like the sign at Big Donut Drive-In. Taryn had never stayed inside someone long enough to see a gaping anus. Watching the last trickles of come pour out, he marveled at his incredible luck. The hole shut and returned to its regular pucker. Every so often, it would burp out some more come.

Shamus Little stared at Taryn Rearden. He had no idea what the muscleman would do next. It made him nervous.

"What"?

"I ain't no fucking fag"!

"I know. Of course not. Do you want me to fuck you again next Saturday?"

"Hell, yes!"

THE SPOTTER

Shamus spent most days at the gym, and his social life revolved around the people he met there. He was short and stocky, with huge arms, legs, and chest. His butt was a work of art. He was huge everywhere except between his legs. There, he was well below average, which was a source of anxiety for him. His balls were standard, but his dick was tiny. He was uncircumcised, adding to his fears of being different down there. In his social circle, most of the guys were cut. The only person who really cared about Shamus's dick size was Shamus himself.

What began as a simple comparison in his teen years evolved into an obsession as he got older. Shamus's sexuality blossomed out of his obsession with size. He avoided guys with little dicks, and started lusting after the guys in the locker room with huge cocks. He'd been with quite a few and got very good at taking even the biggest. He was very fit and caught the eye of many men, some who identified as straight and others who were as gay as Shamus was becoming.

One day, the holy grail walked into the locker room. Garret was a new member with huge muscles and a massive bulge in his workout shorts. It was so big it defied explanation. Shamus wondered if the guy had elephantiasis or some other disorder that caused him to swell up. He didn't want to be obvious, but his eyes kept darting toward Garret's crotch as they worked out beside each other.

Garret smiled at Shamus. "Do you mind spotting me?"

Shamus stood over Garret, catching the weight and gently assisting when Garret asked for his help. The whole time, he stared hungrily at Garret's crotch. The humongous blob of flesh wiggled inside its cloth prison with each lift. Garret caught Shamus staring.

"You like it?" Garret asked.

Shamus nodded. "I want to see it."

"Let's shower." The tall, confident man waltzed into the locker room. The two men took shower stalls across from each other. Garret peeled off the shorts, revealing a cock the size of two coffee cans. It was a bit misshapen, but it was a gigantic dick. Shamus grew weak in the knees looking at it.

Garret smiled. "It's too big for fucking, but I love it when guys worship it." He stepped into the shower and began soaping up the gigantic package.

"Come on, brother, let's see what you got."

Shamus was deeply ashamed of his size. When he removed his sweats, Garret whistled. "Damn, I'm sorry, buddy."

Shamus turned a dark shade of crimson. "It's pathetic," he said.

Garret shook his head. "I used to be smaller. You don't have to be that small if you don't want to."

Shamus couldn't believe his ears. "What do you mean?"

Garret shrugged. "This is silicone. I got it done in Tijuana. You could, too."

A whole world opened up for Shamus in that instant. He could be bigger!

Garret said, "Why don't you come over to my apartment and spend some time up close with it? I need to get off, and you're fucking sexy as hell."

"You mean you don't care about my dick?"

Garret shook his head. "I just need you to hold mine, maybe kiss it a little."

Shamus was rock-hard. His little dick pumped in the air. Garret smiled. "I knew you were the right type. It's hard to find guys who aren't put off by me."

"No way," Shamus said, "I can't fucking believe my eyes. It's beautiful."

The two men toweled off together, dressed, and headed to Garret's place.

It was a shabby apartment near the gym. Garret wasn't a great housekeeper. Most of the surfaces had empty protein shake bottles and dirty dishes. He didn't bother to clean up. He grabbed Shamus's face and kissed him. As Garret explored Shamus's mouth with his tongue, he pressed his waist into the smaller man. Shamus started to drool precum in his sweatpants. The excitement of so much dick pressed up against him was nearly enough to make him come right then.

Garret grabbed Shamus's hand and placed it on the bulge. "Go on, rub it."

Shamus didn't need encouragement. He explored every square inch of the massive lump of meat. His hands reached under and cupped the tip. It must have weighed ten pounds.

"Pull my pants down. Go ahead."

Shamus struggled to get the shorts off. The waistband got hung up on the fat meat. When it finally sprung free, Shamus knelt before the God-like cock. He understood what Garret had meant by "worship." It was a deity of flesh. The impossibly heavy cock began to swell and lift slightly off the man's balls.

Garret took command. "I want you to bury your face in it and tongue my dick."

Shamus could smell the gym soap on the sides of the

massive tunnel. He obeyed. His face couldn't fit in the large opening, but his tongue did. He tasted the tip of the cock, drooling precum, and licked it.

"Oh, yeah, just like that." Garret moaned softly, holding Shamus's head against the opening. Shamus's cock obsession was reaching its apex. He was in heaven. Buried in its tunnel of flesh, the head was churning out more precum.

Garret pulled Shamus's face away from his giant cock and said, "Slow down. I'm close. I want to do more with you."

He pulled Shamus to his feet and lowered his sweats. The little bodybuilder's miniature cock was rigid and throbbing. Droplets of precum emerged and dripped down his shaft.

Shamus said, "What do you want me to do?"

"This." Garret took hold of Shamus's cock and guided it to the fleshy opening of his enormous cock. He put a hand around Shamus's waist and pulled him close. Shamus's little cock slipped inside Garret's. The silicone had caused the foreskin to thicken, which narrowed the opening. Shamus was engulfed by the soft cock-pussy. It gripped him slightly so that as he slid back and forth, fucking Garret's huge dick, he felt each stroke on his shaft and head.

Garret let out a loud breath. "Fuck that's good. Keep going."

Shamus see-sawed in and out. His little dick must have felt like a moth flying in that cavernous opening, but it was enough for Garrett. Both men were building toward orgasm.

Garret shuddered. "Oh fuck, dude, you're gonna make me come."

Shamus was so turned on by the huge dick he was fucking that he forgot to respond. He moaned and grunted, but all language had left him. He shook his head suddenly as if trying to get a fly to leave him alone.

Garret said, "You like my cock-pussy, don't you, boy?"

Shamus nodded. He hadn't even taken a moment to look at Garret's incredible body. Two dark saucer-sized nipples covered his enormous pecs. He reached up and touched one. The teat was thick and fleshy. Shamus rolled it between his fingers.

"Oh fuck, man, you're gonna make me come!" Garret shook with imminent orgasm. When Shamus squeezed the teat hard, Garret let loose. "Aw, man! Here it comes!"

With Shamus lodged inside the opening, a white geyser erupted past his cock, spraying both men with Garret's cum. Beads of sweat formed on Garret's taut skin. Shamus tasted it. If the alpha male could be made into a soft drink, it would taste like Garret.

The sweat was the catalyst for Shamus's orgasm. "Mmmm!" With a loud moan, Shamus shot his load into the opening. The cum blew back in a white spray, coating both men once more in manly essence.

Garret said, "I've been looking for a smaller one like yours. It's the perfect size."

For the first time in his life, Shamus felt proud of his little cock. He said, "If I get silicone like you, maybe I won't fit in there anymore."

Garret gave a wicked grin. "Then I won't tell you my doctor's name."

DIRTY COP

Detective Rocco Pounder and his partner Ash Hunter sat in the unmarked cruiser, dunking plain cake donuts in their coffee. They were staking out a bachelor apartment on Speedway in Venice. The man who lived there, Shamus Little, was a small-time dealer of Quaaludes, Darvon, and anabolic steroids. Word on the street was that he had better prices than his competitors. Rocco and Ash believed those prices meant he was directly connected to a kingpin moving the stuff. They had no interest in arresting Shamus. They wanted information.

Captain Harry Boyle had given Rocco and Ash tremendous leeway on this case. The steroid epidemic in Venice made headlines. Perfectly healthy men were dying from combinations of steroids, alcohol, and narcotics. The two detectives needed to get to the source and put him behind bars. Whoever supplied Shamus was the next rung up the ladder. They hoped he would squeal.

Rocco grew up in the Valley but surfed in Dogtown with the Z-Boys. He had seen Shamus as a teen when he first started going to Muscle Beach in Santa Monica before the pier burned down, and they moved to

Venice. Shamus was always naturally muscular, and lifting weights had made him look great. Big ass, big thighs, v-shaped torso. That was Shamus Little in 1968. In 10 years, he had gone from a sculpted beauty to a 'roided out balding beast. His muscles were obscenely huge and leathery. His face was pockmarked, and his thick, russet hair had thinned and fallen out. Despite his transformation, he still had a handsome square jaw and long eyelashes that could only be described as pretty. And his legendary ass was still huge, although it was striated with muscle now. His huge latissimus dorsi exaggerated the V-shape of his torso. Rocco was on the fence as to whether the muscular gains were worth marring his perfect beauty.

Rocco's partner Ash grew up in El Segundo, or, as the locals called it, "Smell Segundo" because of the sewer treatment facility there. He knew his way around Venice, having biked there a lot as a kid. He had never seen Shamus before last week, so he had no idea how much steroid use had affected him. He just knew that he had to get him to sing so they could move closer to the source.

Rocco Pounder was exceptionally well-endowed. He didn't like the attention, so he used a few tricks to keep his penis from showing. He wore pants two sizes too large and kept his keys and wallet in his left front pocket. When he surfed, he tucked it under and then lodged the rest between his butt cheeks. He had to tie off his trunks high on his waist to keep the shaft tucked. If he wore his trunks low on his waist, either his cock would slide down and find its way out his leg, or the top of his tucked cock would show above the waistline behind him! He had a rough time at Van Nuys High. His nickname was Cock-o Pounder. Boys would neigh like a horse when he walked by. Girls used to corner him and boldly ask him to stick his whopper cock into their tiny vaginas. When he refused, they called him a faggot. When he graduated, he moved to Studio City to avoid those assholes.

Rocco's police uniform was tailored. He begged for a loose fit, but the academy gave him tight, double-knit polyester pants. He couldn't wear his cock down his left leg; it was obscene. He tucked it and wore his pants high. When he made detective, he got big pants, but Captain Boyle said he dressed like a slob. Pounder had to buy form-fitting suit pants. He had recently discovered that a jockstrap two sizes too small would keep his cock tucked and hold his cock head against his lower back. Sitting on his dick all day was uncomfortable. He always volunteered to get the donuts. He encouraged Ash to walk with him on the beat instead of driving.

Ash was oblivious to his partner's battle of the bulge. He admired Rocco's rugged good looks and five o'clock shadow. He imagined how his lips would burn after kissing him for hours. He had no idea how Rocco felt about him. He was just grateful to sit beside him in the car, dunking donuts.

Shamus passed by the cruiser. Rocco dumped his coffee.

"Ash, wait here."

"Shouldn't we go together"?

"I think Shamus will spook if there's two of us. Watch the door; if anyone goes in, you're my backup."

Ash shrugged. He wanted to finish his coffee anyway. He watched Rocco's big ass when he walked away. It was an odd-looking ass, but it was sexy.

The compact, brawny homunculus opened the door and frowned.

"Shamus Little"?

"Yeah."

"I'm Detective Pounder from the LAPD. May I ask you a few questions"?

"Whoa, dude. Rocco Pounder"?

"Yeah."

"You're a Z-Boy! And a cop"?

Rocco hadn't imagined that the self-obsessed body-builder would have ever noticed him over the years. Surfing and bodybuilding rarely mixed.

"You been watching me lift since, like, 1970, right"?

"Uh, well, I noticed you on my way to the water."

"Dude, no, no, no. You sat and watched me before and after low tide."

Rocco blushed. He was busted. "Well, I watched the bodybuilders, yes. You were one of them."

"Did you like what you saw"?

"How did you know my name, anyway"?

"Uh, you're a legend. Cock-o Pounder. They say your dick is so long, you have to tuck it in your ass!"

Rocco felt his cardboard world crashing down. His charade had just made him a worse laughing stock. Some shithead from Van Nuys High must have poisoned the water. He was speechless.

Shamus was high. Rocco guessed it was ludes.

"Dude, is your dick in your ass"? He reached past the detective's gun and felt the shaft of Rocco's gigantic cock lodged between his ass cheeks.

"Holy fuck! You're a goddamn freak of nature!" He moved his hand higher until he found the head poking out of the waistband of the jock strap. "Nice"!

Rocco punched Shamus in the face and pinned him to the wall. Rocco's arms were no match against Shamus's gargantuan muscles. The bodybuilder pushed back, knocking Rocco onto the bed. He quickly straddled the cop and held him pinned.

"What was that for"? Shamus asked.

"I don't like people talking about my cock."

"Shit I didn't know. I'm sorry." Shamus hopped off the detective's abdomen and stood.

"Do you know why I'm here"?

"I'm guessing it's to discuss my part-time business."

Rocco nodded.

"Yeah, well, I'm small time. Are you going to arrest me"?

"Hopefully not. We need your cooperation."

"Who's we"?

"The LAPD, numbskull!"

"You need to relax, brah." Rocco fished a Quaalude off the nightstand.

"I'm not taking a lude, jackass."

Shamus smiled. "If you want my cooperation, I need you to calm down."

Rocco had heard that Quaaludes felt really good. He was curious.

"Here." Shamus poured ice water into a thermos cup.

Rocco was not perfect. He'd seen dirty cops do a lot worse. Ash could drive. He swallowed the lude. "Okay, now you gotta talk."

"Not yet." Shamus went to the bathroom. He was in there for ten minutes or more. Rocco heard water being dumped or sprayed into the toilet. What was Shamus doing?

He knocked, "Shamus, what's going on"?

"I'm washing up."

Shamus opened the door and bumped into Rocco. He was wearing a black posing strap.

"Sorry, Detective Pounder. I was rude. How do you feel"? Shamus rubbed the detective's back and then lowered his hand to his wraparound cock head. Rocco jumped at the touch. It felt different.

"That's the ludes coming on. Do you like it? Shamus polished the knob. It grew.

"Stop. You're touching my dick."

Shamus yanked down the detective's pants. "Part two of my condition, you gotta let me see the legend."

Rocco thought he should feel angry and violent, but he let the muscle imp have his way.

Shamus pulled the tiny jockstrap down to the detective's ankles. Like a flesh pendulum, Rocco's magnificent dick fell from his butt cheeks and swung to the front.

Shamus jumped out of the way of the third leg before it kicked him.

"Motherfuck! That is a wonder of God. You lucky, lucky man."

Rocco couldn't understand why the muscleman's compliment felt so good. He was proud of his manhood for the first time instead of ashamed. "Thanks, man."

Shamus reached into the pouch of his posing strap and fondled himself.

"Cock-o Pounder. I never thought I would see it."

"Does it turn you on"? Rocco never talked about his dick. It had to be the drugs.

"Yeah. It's super long but not too thick."

"It's not done yet." Rocco jerked his cock until it stood at full attention. It gained an inch or two in circumference; the head was the size of a peach.

Shamus kneeled and took the detective's head into his mouth.

Rocco thought, "Stop," but his mouth said, "Oh yeah."

"Let me show you a magic trick." Shamus opened his mouth wider than any human mouth should open. He pushed his head towards Rocco's waist. The colossal cockhead disappeared into his mouth, but then it kept going. The detective watched the entire length of his cock vanish down the muscleman's mouth. He could see the cockhead stretching the throat on its way down. He got even harder. Shamus buried his nose in Rocco's pubic hairs and sucked like a nursing baby. He stayed sucking and swallowing for a long minute and then withdrew with watering eyes and a cough.

Rocco was a virgin. He masturbated once a month. He thought about men, so he figured he might be gay. Shamus confirmed it. After catching his breath, the muscleman went down on Rocco again, holding his face to the groin of the detective he had admired from afar.

The door to the apartment opened, and Ash walked in.

"Hey, Rocco, someone came in the building, and I -"

Rocco was high as fuck now. He didn't care what Ash saw.

"Hey, Ash, come join the party. Have a lude or two!"

Ash stared as Shamus withdrew, revealing each inch of Rocco's schlong. Shamus's throat was a clown car. More and more inches of meat appeared. Ash saw the head move up the throat and out of the mouth, standing free at full attention. Ash had never gotten an erection so fast, not even when he was a youngster.

Ash considered himself well-hung at seven-and-a-quarter inches by six. He had a long fat dick compared to most people. Rocco was in the stratosphere. His cock looked like a velvet rope at a nightclub. It defied gravity.

Rocco extended a hand holding a little pill that read Lemmon 714—a Quaalude.

"Come on, Ash, it feels so fucking good." Shamus put his hand on Ash's bulging hard-on and rubbed it.

Five minutes later, Ash was watching in fascination as Shamus rubbed Crisco on his muscular anus. He succumbed to peer pressure and waited for the ludes to take effect. He spent hours in the car next to Rocco and never once glimpsed the monster he was packing. He felt a tingling sensation in his extremities, sort of like an erection, but in his hands and toes. It was the ludes.

Shamus wasted no time. He unzipped Ash's fly and deep-throated his thick dick. Ash had been with a few scrawny guys who licked at the tip of his cock. He had never felt a mouth take him completely, and he had definitely never felt his cock head slip down someone's throat. Shamus was going to make him cum if he continued. Ash lifted the muscleman's head from his cock. Shamus pushed his lips into Ash's, and they felt each other's tongues. Shamus whispered, "I need you to warm me up."

He undid Ash's belt buckle. Rocco watched, hard as a rock, slowly jerking his meat.

Ash's pants were off, and Shamus, facing him, put the thick cock head against his greased hole. He grimaced as he bore down on the thick dick. It slipped past the sphincter, and in a smooth glide, it filled Shamus's rectum. The head rested against the flesh at the back of the anal canal. Then Shamus started riding a horsey in Ash's lap. He unbuttoned the shirt and put his hand on Ash's nipple.

The Quaaludes were coming on hard now. Ash experienced his entire body as one huge sensitive cockhead. Every touch drove him wild with pleasure.

Rocco came over and put his dick over his partner's shoulder, next to his neck. The cock felt like it weighed twenty pounds. Shamus scooped up Rocco's dick and swallowed it again. Rocco threw his head back. Having Rocco's dick and Shamus's square jaw rubbing on his neck and shoulder made Ash feel like part of a secret club. He didn't mind the saliva dripping on him because every sensation was a mini orgasm.

Shamus was the ringmaster. He got up off of Ash, bent over, and started to blow him. He presented his ass like an orangutan in estrus. "Your turn, Rocco."

"Shamus, it will never fit. I'll hurt you."

"I'm a bodybuilder; I love pain. Now fuck me"! He returned to sucking Ash deeply.

Rocco had fantasized about putting his dick in Shamus since he first came to Muscle Beach. He put the head against the slick hole. His partner was a little thicker than him, so his head went in easy. "Oh, oh god." Shamus used his massive buttocks muscles to push Rocco in further. He stopped worrying and pushed in until he hit the rectum wall. He still had four or five inches to go. He pulled back and settled for a shallow fuck. Shamus pinched tight and pulled Rocco closer. The big guy from the Valley was losing his virginity. He didn't want it to become a bloodbath. Then Shamus twisted to the left, and Rocco passed the rectum into a whole new place. He thrust forward, burying his cock to the hilt. Shamus suppressed screams by pressing his nose into Ash's crotch, blocking the airway. Shamus couldn't breathe, and he liked it.

Ash was fascinated by the amount of muscle he saw. Steroids fuck up your liver and cause deformities, but Shamus wore it all well; he was so handsome that even with some of the less attractive side effects, he was a god. Ash tweaked his nipples. They were like pebbles; they were so hard. Shamus managed to moan. Ash massaged the lats, amazed by their smooth, rigid power.

Rocco looked at the perfectly muscled ass he was fucking. It was heart-shaped, widening to accommodate his girth. He looked at his partner, head thrown back in ecstasy. He longed to be close to him now that they both knew their desires. They locked eyes. Ash leaned forward, and Rocco met him halfway. They explored each other's mouths. The ludes intensified their passion.

"I want you both in me," Shamus announced.

Shamus sat with his back to Ash, impaling himself on the thick cock. Shamus leaned back against Ash. He lifted his powerful legs, presenting a stuffed hole to Rocco. The virgin was really getting some now. He placed his head at the opening. It was standing room only in Shamus's ass. But the bodybuilder picked up a brown bottle and inhaled. His rectum throbbed visibly. "Now!"

Rocco pushed in and slid along his partner's slick,

greasy cock, doubling the width of flesh inside Shamus. He pushed further until he met Ash's cockhead at the back wall. Ash gasped as he felt Rocco turn a corner and keep sliding into the perfect ass.

Rocco thrust back and forth, causing Shamus to wet his posing strap. The man had so little down there. Rocco peeled it back and exposed the tiny cock and average balls. The muscle-bound man's penis was like a leaky faucet. Clear sticky liquid ran from it in droplets. Every so often, it gushed a big stream.

Shamus was on another plane of existence. His eyes showed only the whites. He moaned like a cat in heat. Rocco scooped up some Shamus juice and tasted it. It was sweet and musky. He fed more to Ash and Shamus. Both gobbled like it was gravy.

Ash felt it first. He was going to cum. He whimpered. He reached out and played with Rocco's hairy nipples. That put Rocco over. The two partners, joined together inside this masterpiece of muscle and ass, were going to shoot. Their breath grew shallow and matched pace. They kissed again passionately, knowing their friendship had changed forever. Rocco put a gentle hand on Ash's cheek. The virgin cop buried his tongue in his partner's mouth.

Shamus was a hair trigger. Seeing the two men fall in love while locked inside his ass caused him to ejaculate masses of hot white sperm onto his belly and knees. The squirting was so powerful that both men heard the cum splatter.

Simultaneously, the two men shot their load. Rocco plunged forward until he was completely buried. Ash shot so much cum it squirted out Shamus's stretched hole. Rocco's first orgasm inside a man lasted over a minute. His cum spattered Shamus's colon repeatedly until a teacup's worth of ejaculate was shot deep inside.

Shamus quivered with excitement. He stood and turned so both men saw their dicks slip out. Shamus was open so wide he looked like a donut. Torrents of cum spilled from his ass. Like three pilgrims at the fountain of youth, the men captured the cum in their cupped hands and drank it. Shamus was still open wide when a second batch came from his left colon. Ash and Rocco lay down and caught the spilling cum in their open mouths and all over their face, like a glazed old fashioned. The dilated anus slowly closed shut.

The orgy continued as the three men took turns kissing. Dicks hardened, weed was smoked, and Ash grew bold. "Rocco, I want you to fuck me."

Shamus shouted. "Yes! Let me be your coach. I can get you through it."

Rocco's cock stood at full attention. He wanted to fuck his handsome partner, but he didn't want to hurt him.

Ash applied Crisco to his hole. Shamus inserted two, then three fingers. Ash was an experienced bottom but needed additional stretches, just like a weightlifter. Rocco was enormous. "You can do this, man. I took both your fat cocks at once. It's easy."

Ash nodded. He lay on his back, ass at the edge of the bed, resting his head on Shamus' bent knees.

Rocco stepped to the plate. His cock was bigger and harder than it had ever been. He wished he were like Ash: big but not colossal. He knew this might not go well. But he put the head to Ash's hole and drilled in.

Ash cried out in agony. "Fuck! Ow shit!"

Shamus intervened. "Rocco, stay right there, don't move."

Ash pounded the mattress and tore at the sheets. Rocco wanted so badly to pull away and stop hurting his partner. In a minute, Ash adjusted. He nodded. In one smooth motion, Rocco plunged deep, filling and stretching the rectum with his colossal horse cock.

"Oh. Oh. Shit. Is that it"?

Rocco nodded, but Shamus corrected him. "You need to let your big friend in all the way."

Ash moaned. He was in pain, but it felt so good. His eyes watered, and his heart began beating rapidly. Rocco didn't hurt now. His coach held a small brown bottle under his nose. Shamus nodded at Rocco.

Rocco tore through the second sphincter and conquered the colon.

Ash cried. Tears ran down his cheeks. Rocco started to withdraw, but Shamus shook his head. "Breathe, Ash, Breathe. You're going to need to learn to do this. Your man will never leave you. You hear me? He needs to be deep. You need to take all of your man."

Ash nodded. His head throbbed again as the brown bottle passed under his nose.

"Okay, Rocco. That second sphincter needs to come loose. Fuck it hard with your dickhead."

Rocco pistoned in and out of the colon. Ash screamed at first. In a minute, he was purring like a kitten.

"Go for it, Rocco. My work is done."

With Shamus's blessing, Rocco pounded in and out of his partner with abandon. Ash wailed and moaned, but not from pain. He sniffed the brown bottle a few times.

"Rocco, oh Rocco. I never knew you were so big. You're so goddamn sexy."

Rocco humped his partner and grunted.

"I have wanted you since the day we met in the Academy."

Rocco managed a word. "Really"? The pace of his fucking was furious. He felt rage, sadness, and a dozen other shameful feelings dissolve as he penetrated Ash.

"Did you feel the same"?

Rocco nodded. It wasn't a lie, just easier than explaining his hang-ups because of his monster cock.

"I feel you inside me." Ash put a hand on his flat

belly, where Rocco's cockhead protruded. Ash placed Rocco's hand on the spot. "It's like a baby kicking."

The image of Ash pregnant with his baby was shamefully exciting. He risked it. "I'm gonna make you pregnant tonight."

Ash loved it. "We're making babies. It's going to be quadruplets. Your cock is so big."

Rocco smiled. "You want me to shoot my baby gravy up in your hole"?

"God, yes, fuck me until I conceive. Pour it all over my insides."

It was exciting to talk dirty. So exciting, Rocco became aware of a need to unload. He felt a tongue on his asshole. Shamus had kneeled behind him and was eating his ass. Having a tongue in his hole while he completely filled another felt right. He pretended that Ash was feeling the same, easy feeling in his ass.

Ash felt like he was going to tear open. The constant pain was nothing compared to the satisfaction of being filled by his crush, Rocco, and giving him pleasure. He played with his own long fat cock. The more he thought about pleasing Rocco, the hornier he got. As he imagined what his insides might look like stretched and pounded, he bridged a gap. He started leaking. Rocco saw this and quickened his pace, slamming his hips into Ash with each powerful thrust.

Ash blew a massive load on himself and in Rocco's face. It was squirting in time with Rocco's thrusts. Rocco threw his head back and hollered. "Fuck! Fuck yeah! I'm cumming"!

Globs of semen shot into Ash's behind. Ash put his hand on the pulsating head where it poked up from his belly. He rubbed it, which caused Rocco to cum a second time.

"Ash, fuck! Fuck! You're going to have my butt babies!"

Ash jacked himself hard until he shot his third load

of the day. Rocco collapsed on top of him, still firmly wedged inside. They kissed.

As the minutes ticked by, Rocco couldn't go soft. He had to stop kissing Ash and think about work. That did it. His cock shortened and withdrew from the colon, at which point Ash involuntarily pushed out the huge soft dong. He dripped with semen. Shamus poked his head in and lapped up the semen, cleaning Ash's hole.

Ash felt stretched apart.

Shamus said, "I know you came here to find out my supplier."

Rocco was stoned and high, but he managed to sit up and take note.

"I don't have one. I go to Tijuana and buy the stuff. It's not illegal to bring it back. That's why my prices are low. No middleman."

"So you're responsible for the crisis"?

"No, I am small potatoes. As dealers go, I'm about as big as my dick. You guys are looking for Rocco's dick."

"Yeah, any leads"?

"Talk to Danny Dong in Chinatown. Please don't say I told you."

"You're a confidential informant now, Shamus. We may need to visit you often."

"I'll keep a can of Crisco ready for your call."

"We like it when you squeal."

Back in the car, the two partners were reviewing the night's events. Ash leaned a head on his partner's shoulder. Rocco proudly displayed his snake-like appendage down the left leg of his tight polyester pants. Ash traced circles on the incredible bulge while they talked.

"When you said you were gonna make me pregnant, I almost died of pleasure."

"I shared that muscleman's fuckhole with you. It was crazy."

"I know, we stretched him wide open," Ash remarked.

"Did you see His asshole? It looked like the sign at Randy's Donuts."

"Hey, do we have any donuts left"?

"Nope. And we both need a coffee."

"I'm buying this time."

HARDHATS AND NIGHTSTICKS

※ I ※

SHANE

Shane Biggars was an orphan. Growing up in foster care, he dreamed of working in construction. After finishing high school, he enrolled in a vocational program and started working as a laborer on construction sites. Shane loved building things with his hands.

For several years, Shane worked hard and proved himself a skilled and reliable worker. He climbed the ranks and eventually landed a foreman job overseeing a team of loyal workers on a skyscraper construction project in Downtown Los Angeles. It was his first high-rise project, and he was delighted to be the foreman on something so important.

However, there was one thing that made Shane's job more challenging than it should have been - he had been born with an enormous penis. This may seem like a blessing to the small or average man, but his cock was so long, thick, and heavy that it was challenging for him to balance on beams and carry out certain other tasks on the job site.

Shane was aware of his big problem since he started showering in school. He had developed strategies to keep it hidden. He had to wear baggy, oversized dungarees to hide his abnormality. Managing a team of young men wasn't easy. One slip-up and he would be the butt of those jokes he'd left behind in high school locker rooms. He managed to keep his massive secret under wraps but couldn't hide his lack of balance and coordination. Even his best friend, the charming and handsome Charlie Watts, was unwilling to work with him.

"Shane, you and me are pals, but I got kids. If you slip up there, it could send us both tumbling."

Shane knew he was right. "You're a good friend, Charlie. A bad friend wouldn't have the courage to tell it straight."

Charlie sipped his coffee. "Yeah, you can count on me to have your back, even if it hurts."

An image appeared in his mind's eye. Handsome Charlie stood behind Shane, putting his dick in his ass. It hurt. He shook his head as though it would banish the thought from his mind. It lingered, the image of Charlie holding Shane's bottom steady while he penetrated his tight asshole. His monster started to swell. He didn't dare let Charlie discover what was hidden so well in those baggy pants.

"Gotta pee."

He leaped up and ran to the port-a-potty. He locked the door, pulling out his stiffening cock while it could still bend. He had to stand against one wall and lift the cock at an angle so it could grow to its full length. Masturbating took hours, and he didn't have time. Desperate for a distraction, he looked down into the blue water, filled with toilet paper and a foul odor. It was enough. He felt the flow of blood change direction, and the two-foot pole softened. He carefully stuffed it back into his pants. He avoided Charlie for the rest of that day.

Shane was aware of his big problem since he started showering in school. He had developed strategies to keep it hidden. He had to wear baggy, oversized dungarees to hide his abnormality. Managing a team of young men wasn't easy. One slip-up and he would be the butt of those jokes he'd left behind in high school locker rooms. He managed to keep his massive secret under wraps but couldn't hide his lack of balance and coordination.

The boss, Nick Martinez, started to receive complaints from other workers about Shane's performance. Some of them claimed that he was a safety hazard, and they were concerned that his balance issues could lead to accidents on the job site. Most of the guys liked Shane, but none wanted to fall to their death because he couldn't hold his own on the high beam.

One day, Nick called him into his office to discuss the complaints. Nick was fond of Shane and knew this would be a difficult conversation.

"Biggars, you know why I called you in here?"

Shane shook his head, even though he had an idea.

Nick said, "Some guys tell me you're losing your balance. It means I gotta take you off the high beams. Are you cool with working in the office?"

Shane wasn't. He did his best to hide the pain and anger. He mustered up some humor. "Does it mean I'll be staring at your ugly mug all day?"

Nick laughed. "Okay, it's settled. Until you get your balance back, you're managing the books."

Shane groaned inwardly. He took up construction because his intelligence lay in his hands, not his head. He could add up numbers, but he wasn't any good with fractions, percentages, or anything like algebra. He knew it was a matter of time before Nick realized Shane was a poor fit for that job.

As though he had read Shane's mind, he said, "Don't worry, I got a construction accountant. He'll report to you. He knows how to do all the grunt work. You just gotta manage him good."

As if on cue, a slightly built young man sauntered

into the office and lay a stack of papers in front of Nick.

"Here, sign these purchase orders."

Nick smiled. "Walter, this is our foreman, Shane. He'll be signing all your POs and checks going forward. Don't worry; he don't bite."

Shane extended a meaty paw, and young Walter shook it gently. The boy studied the hulking construction worker, looking below the waist for a while. Shane was unnerved.

When Walter returned to the accounting bullpen, Nick closed the adjoining door.

He said, "Shane, I'm not supposed to ask, and you don't have to answer. But have you been to the doctor about your balance problem? It could be something serious, and I don't want to see you get sick."

Shane shook his head. He felt comfortable around Nick, but not enough to reveal his massive problem. But he was nervous and didn't want to leave the question unanswered.

"I know what the problem is. I'm not sick. It's something else."

Nick leaned forward. "What do you mean? What did the doctor say?"

Shane was in over his head. He trusted Nick, but maybe not enough to reveal his secret. He debated it. Fuck it.

Shane hooked a thumb in his waist behind the top button. "I think it's better if I show you the problem."

Nick frowned, but he leaned in, curious. "Go on."

Shane unbuttoned his pants and let them drop, revealing the colossal log that ran down his right thigh. Even soft, it nearly reached his knee.

The boss nearly fell out of his chair. "Holy shit! Holy fuckin' shit! Put that away!"

Shane pulled up his trousers, adjusted his meat so it wouldn't show, then buttoned up.

Shane said, "Please don't talk about it, okay?"

Nick's mouth hung open. "How do you get laid with that thing?"

Shane regretted sharing his secret. Whatever relief he felt was eclipsed by his annoyance and anger at having to go through the usual big dick questions.

"I don't. It's too big."

Nick stood and put a paternal arm on Shane's shoulder. "I'm sorry, man. I was out of line. I got a big one, but it's nothing like yours." Nick put a firm hand on his thigh, exposing a much larger-than-average cock, swelling and stretching against the fabric.

Shane said, "Are you getting hard?"

Nick nodded and blushed. "Sorry, man, you see a dick that big, and your body just goes into autopilot. Shit! It's stuck."

Indeed, the lump looked trapped in Nick's tight polyester pants.

Shane said, "What are you gonna do?"

Nick grabbed Shane by the arm and pulled him into the bathroom, locking it. "You can say no. Will you suck me off?"

Shane was stunned. He'd lived the life of a monk his whole life. No woman would touch him. He'd never even thought about sex with men. The thought used to make him sick, but looking at his handsome boss, desperate to get off, he felt no disgust, only a mixture of curiosity and lust. He nodded.

Nick said, "You done this before?"

Shane shook his head.

Nick smiled. "You lucked out; I'm a good teacher. You're gonna love this."

The boss pushed Shane's shoulders until the big foreman kneeled before him. Nick peeled the tight stretchy pants down until half his cock was exposed. Shane reached forward and helped, pulling from further down the trouser leg so the fabric slid easily over the massive lump. Suddenly, Nick's fat hog broke free from his trousers, smacking Shane hard on the chin. They both laughed.

Nick took command. "I wanna see you jacking off while you suck me. Take your pants off."

Just hearing those words made Shane's cock swell with desire. Something was intoxicating about a father figure like Nick admiring his anatomy and giving him orders. He pulled his pants to his ankles, revealing his rapidly hardening cock. Nick's eyes grew wider as Shane grew to an absurd size.

Nick said, "Relax your jaw and let your mouth hang open. Don't hold it open; just let it hang. Don't worry if you drool; it's natural."

Shane relaxed obediently, letting his mouth fall open. Nick stepped forward, aiming his cock at the foreman's face. The head was bigger around than the shaft. The foreskin stretched and strained against Nick's lengthening pole until you could no longer tell he was uncircumcised. The throbbing head found its way inside Shane's soft, wet mouth.

It tasted like a mixture of fish and papaya. The odor wasn't unpleasant; it made Shane's mouth water.

Nick exhaled loudly. "Oh, there you go." He gently rocked his hips, letting the fat head slide past Shane's teeth.

"You like that?"

Shane did. His mouth was full, so he just nodded.

Nick was a good teacher. "I'm going to the next level now. You're gonna feel me go in further, and you might need to puke. Try to relax and let your body do its thing."

Shane felt the tangerine-sized head touch his tonsils. His gag reflex kicked in. He retched and convulsed, but Nick held him by the ears and kept pressed there. Tears fell down his cheeks, but he wasn't sad. After a minute or so, the gagging became less constant.

"Good boy. You're doing great. Jack your cock. It makes it easier."

Shane hated his cock. He hated masturbating because it was so massive his arms hurt. But Nick was right; the pleasure centers in the root of his meat sent soothing waves of erotic pleasure throughout his body, including his throat.

Nick caressed Shane's scruffy beard. "I'm moving, okay?"

He didn't wait. He pulled back, then rammed his cock to the back of Nick's throat. He did it fast a dozen times or more. Shane gagged once or twice and even spit up, but he felt good. He felt proud that Nick was using his mouth to get off. Shane liked this, and he would gladly do it again. But then Nick scared him.

"Shane, I'm gonna go all the way now. Alright? Relax and just let it happen." Nick wrapped his big hands around Shane's head, interlacing his fingers. He pushed hard. Shane's eyes watered, and he flailed. "Shh...shh... relax."

Suddenly, Nick's big cock head popped past the tonsils and down Shane's throat. Shane could feel it sliding back and forth behind his Adam's apple.

Nick said, "Tap my leg when you need air. Be quick, though." He held Shane's nose against his pubes and pumped his cock in the foreman's soft throat. "Oh man, Shane, you're a natural. Way better than Walter."

Shane took in this information with a mixture of shock and pride. Walter did this too? The room was turning red. He needed air, even though he wanted Nick inside him as long as possible. Being connected to him like this was like having the father he'd never known. Consciousness was dimming; he tapped Nick's leg.

Nick pulled back, allowing Shane two big gasps and the opportunity to upchuck a thick, clear liquid before forcing his way back down the throat. Shane felt it this time. His throat was sore from the friction, even with all that goop his salivary glands produced. But he loved providing Nick with this service. His cock was magnificent, rivaling anything Shane had seen besides his own, which wasn't even a cock so much as a third leg. He sucked and nursed, wrapping his lips around the thick shaft. He used his tongue to rub the underside of Nick's big, veiny cock.

"Oh shit, yeah. Keep doing that. And jack your dick!" He switched to a long stroke, his cock filling Shane's mouth before plunging forward down his throat, then back.

Shane had forgotten to take care of his meat, which was so hard, it actually defied gravity and lifted off the floor a little. In his mind, it was a sandbag, an albatross: a burden. He didn't feel quite the same now that it served a purpose. As he stroked it, he could taste Nick's juices in his mouth. Nick was staring down at the monstrosity. With each stroke, Shane felt a tingling connecting his throat to his cock. Nick's head tickling his tonsils made jerking his cock more pleasant. In fact, it was the best he'd ever felt about his dick. Nick's obvious obsession was a source of pride.

Suddenly, the nerves connecting his cock to his throat sent pulses that caused his throat to involuntarily contract, stroking Nick's meat in waves.

"Holy fuck, Shane! Puta madre! You're fuckin' amazing!"

Shane heard the words, but he was somewhere else. The throat contractions were just an external symptom of the ecstatic pleasure coursing through his body. He didn't know it, but he was having a throat orgasm. Nick's strokes grew longer and longer until the head almost fell out of Shane's mouth. He was able to take a breath on each outstroke, and they fell into a comfortable rhythm.

Shane felt it first. For the first time in his life, he

felt a genuine, happy wave of orgasmic pleasure running from his crotch to the tip of his cock. He gushed clear precum all over the bathroom floor.

Nick said, "Oh, that's fucking hot. I'm gonna come."

But Shane beat him to it. The first of a dozen loads flew across the bathroom, hitting the mirror behind Nick. Nick heard the splat; that was all he needed to soar over the edge.

"Aaargh! I'm coming!" He pulled Shane's cheeks to his hips, buried as deep inside the foreman's throat as he could go. Shane didn't have to swallow; Nick pumped the hot cum directly down his esophagus. He stayed buried there, spurting ounces of thick cum in waves. Shane saw red. Nick pulled back, giving Shane air just in the nick of time. The boss's cock was still pumping. Shane tasted his first mouthful of cum. It was so good that his cock shot one more massive load, messing up the bathroom floor.

Nick let his softening cock fall, hitting his thigh with a loud "thwack!"

"Shane, you are a natural. I've never had head so good. I hope we can do this again."

Shane stood. He hugged the boss, who pushed him back. "Dude, I ain't no faggot. Knock it off!"

Shane was hurt. He didn't know exactly what it meant to be a faggot, but he wasn't whatever that was. Not the way Nick said it. He just wanted to hug a man the way a son hugs his father.

"Get back to work. Walter will show you the ropes."

Nick threw a bunch of paper towels on the floor and left them for the poor janitor to mop up later. When they left the bathroom, Walter stood with his hand on one hip, glaring at both of them. He shoved a wad of papers at Shane. "These have to be signed by the end of the day. You got something on your lip."

Shane wiped a stray trickle of cum from his mustache. He eyed Walter, who turned tail and swished out of the boss's office.

Nick smiled. "Don't mind him. He's jealous; I usually give him his afternoon feeding about this time."

Shane reviewed and signed the paperwork, making sure the figures looked right. He had a manual calculator at his new desk but didn't know how to use it, so he was just eyeballing and doing his best. Multiplication wasn't really something he could do well in his head, and he was worried this job wouldn't last long.

Walter sat beside Shane. "I'm sorry I was rude. I couldn't help but overhear your talk with Nick about your "problem." I'm sorry you have to deal with that. I have the opposite problem.

Shane turned and smiled. "Can you show me how to use this thing?"

Walter patiently instructed Shane to punch the keys and pull the handle when he was ready to calculate. He got out an old textbook called "Ten Key By Touch" and left it with him. Walter wasn't a bad guy. Shane's curiosity was piqued by Walter's confession. He turned around in his chair and said, "Can I see your problem? I'll show you mine."

Walter stood. "On the count of three, drop your pants."

When Walter's pants fell, they revealed a microscopic penis and mouse balls nestled in a bush of pubic hairs.

Shane struggled to get his pants down past his swelling cock. He bent double, loosening it from the legs down. When he stood straight, Walter sucked air between his teeth.

"Christ on a cross! How do you even walk with that thing?"

He put a hand over his mouth, realizing he had just insulted his boss.

Shane shrugged. "How do you fuck women with that?"

Walter frowned. "That hurts."

"We're even."

The two men stared in fascination at each other's incredibly different appendages. It would be easy to say you could fit a hundred Walter-sized dicks inside Shane's massive pole with room to spare. Even rock-hard, he was less than an inch in length and girth.

Walter stepped forward, wrapping his palm along the underside of Shane's pole. It was nearly too heavy to lift.

Walter said, "The Lord giveth and the Lord taketh away." He raised the cock to his lips. It was so long that he didn't even need to bend. He kissed the massive head, sending shivers down Wayne's spine.

The big-dicked foreman hadn't had sex before today,

and now he was headed for his second time in under an hour.

Walter ran his tongue under the foreskin, cleaning the residue from the earlier encounter. He slurped greedily, making Shane's knees buckle from the intense pleasure.

Walter was a small guy in every way. There was no way he could suck Shane off, let alone take his dick.

Walter lay on the desk, his legs pointed skyward. "Come here." He pulled Shane's cock between his thighs. "Hold my ankles together. The thighs formed a vise, holding Shane's cock tightly.

Instinctively, Shane began thrusting his cock between Walter's thighs. The head punched Walter's chin a few times before Shane lowered his hips and pulled the ankles towards him, sending his cock in an upward trajectory away from the tiny boy's face.

Walter squirmed, his tiny penis leaking precum like a drippy faucet. Shane's heavy cock couldn't help but rub up against the little dick.

Walter moaned with delight. "Oh, Shane, oh god, you're so big! I can't believe my eyes!"

Shane was fascinated by Walter's little dick but wasn't sure he should say anything. He moved his hands down to the lad's shins to increase the pressure against his cock. He felt a gurgling sensation building in his balls.

Without warning, Walter shot a thick load of cum in the air, landing on his chest and face. "Damn, Shane. No hands."

Seeing Walter cum without hands was beautiful. Walter gathered up the cum and rubbed it on his thighs, making a slippery hole for Shane's cock. The added lubrication felt good. Shane surprised himself. He felt the churning in his balls and the pulsing pressure at the base of his cock. His balls drew up tight, and a massive load of cum shot out of his cock. It flew past

Walter's head and landed in a pile of purchase orders. He didn't care. He was absorbed in the moment. Beads of perspiration ran down his forehead, falling on Walter's thighs. Walter ran a finger through the sweat and put it in his mouth.

"Ooh! Such a manly taste."

Shane cracked a smile. "Thanks. I made it myself."

CHARLIE

The next day, Shane had a frog in his throat. Nick had really stretched him out. In a gravelly voice, he said, "Good morning, boss."

Nick grinned. "I'll make you a cup of tea with honey."

Shane said, "Yeah, it hurts. That sounds good."

Nick grabbed his crotch. "The best cure for a sore throat is the hair of the dog that bit you." He pushed Shane into the bathroom.

A blow job on a sore throat first thing in the morning was not Shane's idea of a good start to the day. He still loved the work. Nick's cock made his mouth water just looking at it. When puberty struck Shane many years earlier, he felt the intense urge to procreate. Like many guys in high school, he tried to act on those urges, only to be rejected. He cringed whenever he thought of Alicia Bennett screaming, "No fucking way," and running out of his bedroom. She was a horrible gossip. Plenty of girls wanted to see it, but none would dare let that monster invade them. It was a traumatic coming of age. Shane gave up on sex altogether, never realizing he could make a guy like Nick happy and get off in the process. In truth, he'd only seen the tip of the iceberg. So much sex awaited him if he was willing to experiment. Women no longer interested him. He wanted sex with men.

Sometimes Shane wished he had a smaller dick. Not a lot smaller, just enough to keep his balance and get a blow job or fuck an ass. Walther's thighs were a pretty good substitute, but he wanted a deeper connection. Walter was unyielding when it came to butt fucking.

"Shane, your cock is fucking amazing, but it would leave me wrecked. I'm saving this ass for the right man, and he's a lot smaller than you."

The words stung, but they rang true. Walter was a nice guy with a perfect little nipple of a penis, but there was no connection there. The sex was hollow.

Office work left Shane restless. Whenever Walter had a question for the men onsite, Shane took the job from him. He missed his buddies, especially Charlie Watts. Carrying a purchase order with an error to the site, Shane pondered the irony of his situation. Men would kill to have a huge cock, but they would soon regret having what Shane had. He felt like a Prince complaining about the disadvantages of royalty. When it came to man-on-man sex, cock was king. But Shane had a dictator, a despot between his legs.

He looked for a familiar face when he got to the job site. Charlie Watts came running up to him.

"Hey, if it isn't Shane, Nick's pet! How is office life treating you?"

Shane shook his head. "I miss it out here." He looked up. The skyscraper had grown 200 feet since he'd left.

"Big, eh?"

Shane smiled. "Huge."

Charlie laughed. "That's what they all say, now."

Shane felt the blood rush to his head. "Who says what?"

Charlie patted Shane's leg. "We heard about your little problem."

Shane was furious. His anger filled the air like a cloud of angry hornets. Charlie took a step back. "Oh shit, Shane. I wouldn't have teased you if I knew you were sensitive about it. You're my friend."

Shane took a series of calming breaths. "Charlie, you always tell it like it is. You're the best friend a man could ask for."

Charlie's eyes kept darting downwards. Shane understood. The curiosity must have been killing him.

Charlie said, "Let's you and me have lunch. I got a lot to tell you anyway."

They went to the nearby submarine sandwich shop and shared a giant grinder.

Charlie took a bite of his massive sandwich. With his mouth full, he said, "I got news; my wife, Britney, left me, and she took the kids."

Shane felt pain. It hurt him to think of his good friend suffering. "Oh shit, man. That's awful."

Charlie shrugged. "It was bound to happen. We weren't on the same page about anything."

Shane said, "What happened, though?"

Charlie blushed. "It's kinda embarrassing."

"You don't have to be embarrassed with me, Charlie."

The handsome man nodded. "You're right. You and me don't need secrets. Promise me this doesn't go any further than this table."

Shane nodded.

"Okay. The other day, my wife walked in on me while I was in the middle of...." He hesitated.

"Go on, I'm listening."

Charlie sighed. "You're gonna judge me."

Shane put a hand on Charlie's shoulder. "No judgments."

Charlie said, "Okay. Well, a couple years ago, my

lady stuck her finger in my ass when we were fucking. It was the best feeling in the world. I shot so hard that she probably got pregnant all week. That's when we had the triplets. She never did it again."

Shane had expected a story about drugs or alcohol, not this. "Go on. I'm listening."

Charlie took a long sip of his Coke. "Okay, so I wanted that feeling again. I went to the bookstore, and I saw all those dildos and butt plugs. I bought the extra-small plug and took it home. I kept it hidden under my toolbox in the garage. I stuck that thing up my ass every chance I got. I wore it to work a lot. At first, it hurt, but it didn't take long until it wasn't enough. "

Shane sat up. "Go on."

"So, I went back, and I bought a set. It went from small to extra-large. I worked my way up. It was hard to keep them hidden, so I built a secret cupboard in the garage to hold them."

Shane was intrigued. "Does it really feel good?"

Charlie nodded emphatically. "My dick dripped so hard at work, I had to wear a maxi-pad."

"So Britney walked in on you with the butt plug?"

Charlie shook his head. "Worse. I ain't done. So I wondered if there was something bigger than the extra-large. My ass was getting looser and looser. I was afraid that huge thing would fall out while I was at work. That's when I started looking at the dildos. I wasn't into dick, so I never thought about those realistic-looking things. A butt plug wasn't a dude. But they had some rubber dicks that turned me on. There was one that was three feet long with a giant plug at the base. I bought that. And there was an even thicker one that wasn't made like a plug. You had to ride it up and down."

Shane saw where this was headed. "So Britney caught you with that one. The one you ride up and down."

Charlie nodded. "She called me a fucking pervert and grabbed her suitcases and moved back in with her mom. I miss her and the kids something awful, but now when I get home, it's just wild ass stuffing from sundown to bedtime."

Hearing this got Shane aroused. "I think it's great that you have a hobby."

They both laughed. Charlie wiped a tear or two from his eyes. He was hurting from the breakup.

Shane said, "I can see it hurts."

Charlie chuckled. "Oh, those tears aren't about Britney or the kids. When I laugh, it hurts way up inside."

Shane put down his sandwich. "Are you saying you have that giant plug up your ass right now?"

Charlie put a finger to his lips. "Keep it down, dipshit!" The shop had filled up with coworkers on break.

"Sorry, I wasn't thinking."

Charlie winked and put a hand on Shane's leg. "So you want to come over for supper?"

❧ 4 ❧
SHANE LOSES HIS VIRGINITY

Shane's hand trembled as he rang the doorbell.
Charlie answered the door in a leather get-up. He put an arm around Shane and gave him a half-hug. Shane could feel him shaking, too. They were both jumpier than cats at a tap dance.

"Make yourself at home. Brew?"

Shane said, "Yeah. Whatever you got."

When Charlie turned to go to the kitchen, Shane got an eyeful. Charlie was wearing a jockstrap under assless chaps. His bubble-butt wiggled as he walked. Shane felt his meat strain against his trousers. He couldn't believe this was happening. And with his best friend!

Charlie returned with two Lucky Lagers and sat on the earth-tone sofa beside his friend. They toasted.

Charlie put a hand on Shane's left leg and rubbed. Shane grinned. "I wear it on the right."

"Switch sides."

They rearranged themselves, and Charlie put his hand over Shane's right thigh. He felt the contours of the throbbing meat. His eyes widened as he moved towards the knee, then beyond.

"Holy shit, Shane! What the fuck?" He got to the

end and caressed the colossal head. "They call the boss Nick the Dick, but you got him beat by a mile."

Shane felt a surge of jealousy. "Has he fucked you?"

Shane shook his head. "Nah, he wanted me to blow him. He took it out, but when I asked him to fuck me instead, he put it back. He's got hang-ups."

Shane drained his bottle and leaned back into the sofa, letting his best friend's hands do good work. A spot appeared on his pant leg.

"I gotta see it." Charlie unbuttoned Shane and pulled the waist down over his flat ass.

Shane shook his head. "You gotta pull from the cuffs now. It's too big."

Charlie licked his lips. "That's the hottest fucking thing I ever heard." He got down on his knees like a preacher at a foot washing and tugged on the pant legs. Shane lifted to allow the fabric to slide under him. As Charlie pulled, the base of the big cock came into view. Charlie stopped.

"Oh god, it's bigger than a fire extinguisher! Oh shit, I might come right now." Charlie's jockstrap was stretched. His dick was big enough to tuck under his balls, the way most men wore a jock. It was the perfect size for making babies. No wonder he had so many of them!

Shane watched his friend grow more and more enthusiastic as he pulled the legs of the trousers down, revealing inch after inch of colossal meat. His face eager grin slowly dissolved into a wide-eyed grimace. "Fuck, that's big."

Shane rolled his eyes. He knew it was too good to be true. He grabbed the waist of his pants and tried to pull them up, but Charlie held them in a tug-of-war.

"What are you doing?"

Shane said, "It's okay. I can see you're not up for it. Nobody is."

Charlie scoffed. "Are you fucking kidding me? This is the holy fucking grail, Shane. It's a dream come true."

Shane felt a stab of pent-up sadness pierce his heart. He'd never in his life been told his dick was suitable for sex. He wanted to believe his friend, but he couldn't. He was so used to rejection that his mind couldn't handle it.

Charlie knew Shane pretty well. He probably sensed what was happening. "Dude, I promise you won't be disappointed. Trust me."

Shane closed his eyes as the pants continued their downward journey. As they passed the knee, he heard Charlie gulp. He opened his eyes.

Charlie had his dick out, jacking it slowly. "Oh, my god. Oh, sweet Jesus. Christ on a cracker." His eyes were saucers.

At last, Shane's cock broke free, flying skyward despite its incredible weight.

Charlie shivered. "Where have you been all my life?"

Shane had given up on ever hearing such praises. He'd heard plenty of compliments, but none that were filled with desire like Charlie's.

Shane hadn't noticed the huge can of Crisco tucked behind the table lamp. Shane took a massive handful and lovingly applied it from tip to base on Shane's meat, stroking it, whispering to himself. Shane was overjoyed.

Charlie took a smaller second helping of the creamy white shortening and applied it to his butthole. He slipped a few fingers past the loose flaps that formed a pout. He wiped the rest on his hard cock, making it slick and shiny.

Charlie stood on the sofa, facing Shane. Slowly, he lowered himself over the towering cock with a head as big as a grapefruit. The first inch went in easily before it grew too wide. Charlie strained, pushing downward, until, with a loud pop, the corona snapped past the sphincter.

"Unhhh!" Charlie made an involuntary grunt that any guy into ass-play would recognize. It was a mixture of shock, surprise, pain, and intense pleasure. Shane hadn't heard it before.

"Are you okay?"

Charlie put a finger to Shane's lips. "Don't worry about me. Enjoy yourself."

Shane closed his eyes. He heard Charlie strain and felt his downward push. It stopped a few more inches later. That was it. The remaining inches of Shane's cock, and there were many, felt cold and left out of the fun. Charlie bounced up and down a few times, which felt incredible.

Shane felt sad. He had dreamed it would be different. He hadn't realized there was a limit. Most men probably never reached it, and he doubted Charlie could. But it wasn't nearly enough for Shane.

Then a miracle happened. Charlie lifted his leg and twisted. There was forward movement. Not much, not enough, but a little. Then, with the sound of a hand clap, Shane popped past an opening into a soft, squishy place. Charlie cried out.

Shane said, "Oh god, I poked a hole in you!"

Charlie shook his head. "No, you didn't."

Shane relaxed as Charlie slid easily downward another twelve inches or more. Then the fireworks went off. As Shane rounded another corner, it touched off a nerve inside Charlie.

"Oh fuck, here it comes!"

Charlie's insides were pulsing in waves moving in two directions. They amplified as they crashed into each other. Charlie seized up, doubled over, and straightened, crying, "Yes! Yes! Oh, fuck! Oh, fuck!"

Shane was astonished by the convulsions, but it didn't matter. Those waves were like a hundred tiny hands rubbing up and down all but the last three inches of his dick. Charlie was hovering, but he had no more room to sit down. It shouldn't matter to Shane, but it did. Then his cock head turned a different corner, one that rose upward, and Charlie crash-landed on his lap. They were eye-to-eye. Charlie's mouth opened and closed like a landed sea bass. Shane felt an intense connection with this man. Not only was he his best friend, but he was also something more, something new.

Without thinking, he said, "I love you, man." He leaned forward and kissed Charlie. Charlie kissed back. He held Shane's head and forced his tongue into the depths of his mouth. The kiss lasted several minutes, during which Charlie shook and squeezed, bringing Shane along on the road to orgasm.

Charlie pulled back, studying Shane's eyes like they were an Economics textbook before an exam. "Fuck me. I want you to fuck me."

Charlie grabbed Shane's shoulders, rolled to one side, then onto his back. Shane, wedged firmly inside his friend, landed on top. Charlie pulled his knees to his ears. Shane instinctively put his hands on the soles of Charlie's feet for support.

"Yeah, like that. Just like that." Charlie's eyes disappeared inside his forehead.

Shane pulled back, then let gravity force his cock to snake its way inside his friend.

"Oh, Sweet Jesus! Mother fucking Mary!"

The blasphemy made the moment even more intense. Shane pulled back again, then fell into his friend. Charlie wrapped his hands around Shane's butt, and the next time he pulled back, Charlie shoved him hard.

"Oh yeah. Like that. Right there. Like that."

Shane understood. It wasn't enough to fall; he had to thrust. His hips were genetically programmed to thrust. It was an ancient part of his brain that took over, forcing him to rut Charlie like he was a bitch in heat.

Charlie's cries were equal parts agony and ecstasy.

"Ow! Oh, fuck! Oh yeah! Yes! Yes! Right there! Oh god, right there! Ow! Shit!"

Harder and harder, Shane fucked with wild abandon. It was better than he had imagined. His whole cock was enveloped in flesh, sliding and thrusting ever harder into his dear friend. They kissed again. With each thrust, Charlie grunted swear words into Shane's mouth, but their tongues continued to explore one another.

Charlie's cock had shriveled, but it gushed precum. Shane watched in fascination as it swelled, then deflated, in a cycle that matched the rhythm of Shane's fucking. The deeper he went, the smaller Charlie's dick got. But then it switched. Each deep thrust caused Charlie to swell. At the same time, Shane noticed his stomach rose. He realized the lump was his cock pressing against Charlie's abdomen.

"Oh man, I'm close." Charlie looked dreamily into Shane's eyes. One hand slowly stroked his meat, which was rock hard and pulsing.

Hearing those words and seeing Charlie aroused sent Shane over the edge.

"Me too. Oh fuck, here it comes."

He held himself inside his friend as far as he could, pushing so hard that the lump in Charlie's belly became a small hill. Then the hill throbbed, and Shane released his warm, manly cum inside his best friend.

Charlie groaned. His cock shot ounce after ounce of baby gravy into the air. If a woman were in the room, she would merely need to spread her legs to get pregnant. But it was two men. One load hit Shane's open mouth. He tasted the savory sperm and swallowed.

Exhausted, he collapsed on top of his friend. Charlie nibbled on his earlobe and whispered, "Same time tomorrow?"

5

PINK SLIP

S hane spent the night at Charlie's, and the two drove to work together.

Charlie smiled at Shane. "I won't hear my farts for a week."

When Shane dropped his friend at the site, he noticed he walked with a limp. Shane ignored the wave of self-recrimination for injuring his friend. Whatever pain Charlie felt, Shane was sure it was worth the experience the night before. He felt a rush of warmth in his chest. He had never felt anything like it. Was it love?

When Shane got to the office, Nick said, "You're late. Get me a coffee."

Shane brought a cup of the nasty beverage to his boss. Nick looked him up and down. "Something's different about you."

Shane shrugged. "Nah."

Nick said, "Let me serve you breakfast."

Shane got down on his knees in the bathroom and opened his mouth wide. He had become comfortable with Nick's huge cock in his mouth. Nick pumped in and out on a small river of thick saliva. It dribbled down Shane's chin and puddled on the floor.

"Walter's getting mad. He's hungry, and you're eating all his meals."

Shane felt guilty. Walter was a nice guy. So was Charlie. Sucking Nick's dick was cheating and stealing. He didn't care. He liked being a servant to Nick's giant cock. He fumbled with his trousers and pulled out his cock, stroking it to its full size. He had to reach around Nick's leg to stroke it.

Soon the familiar taste of precum signaled that Nick was close. Shane closed his eyes and let the salty brew flow down his gullet. Nick didn't wait for Shane to come. He pulled his leg out from the space between Nick's forearm and cock, zipping his pants.

"Do it in the sink. I'm sick of cleaning up after you."

Shane did as he was told, wiping the cum from the edges of the sink with a wad of paper towels while washing the rest down the drain.

That day, a strange parade of hard hats made their way to the trailer to talk to Nick. Each one stopped off at Shane's desk, trying to catch a glimpse of his legendary meat. Earl Porter, a chubby, feminine guy, was bold.

"Can I see it? Everyone's talking about it."

Shane was taken aback. "What are they saying?"

"That it's huge."

Shane hoped Charlie hadn't talked about their night of passion.

"That's all?"

Earl wrinkled his nose. "Should there be anything else? Okay, it's not just huge; it's bigger than an elephant trunk. That's what Walter said."

So it was Walter, the little snitch! "No, nothing else."

"So, can I see it?" Earl licked his lips.

"Sure." Shane hauled out his impressive soft cock and plopped it on the desk.

"Holy crap! Oh god! Oh god!" Earl was way too loud.

Nick came running in. "What's wrong?" He saw the cock on the desk, and his face turned red.

"Put that fucking thing away, you freak!" Nick stormed out of the office once Shane put his meat back in his pants.

Earl patted his chest. "Oh god, Shane, I'm sorry. I couldn't help it. That's a beautiful thing you have, and I hope someday you find someone who can fully appreciate it."

Shane nodded. He thought maybe he already had. He wondered if Charlie was willing to give it another go. "Don't worry about it, Earl. It makes everyone scream."

Earl smiled. He was a sweet guy, really. He took a lot of shit from the guys. They bullied him and called him "faggot" and "queer," but he kept on working. Shane wondered if some of those guys didn't secretly fuck him in the port-a-potty after hours. There were a lot of hypocrites working with an otherwise swell bunch of guys. "I mean it, Shane. You deserve it. I never met a nicer foreman."

Earl left. Within minutes, another knock at the door. It was Nick. Walter tagged along behind him, holding a pink envelope.

"Shane, I'm sorry, but I have to let you go."

Shock washed over Shane's face. "What? What did I do?"

Nick shrugged. "You can't just pull your dick out at your desk, Shane. You're not an animal. We can't tolerate that kind of behavior here."

Shane was outraged. "You mean it's okay to fuck my face in the bathroom, but no dicks on the desk? Can I see the terms and conditions of my contract? I want to see where that's written."

Nick punched Shane hard. "Take that back, you fucking faggot!"

Shane stood. He was taller than Nick. His hands curled into fists.

Nick said, "Hit me, and I'll call the cops."

Walter got between them. "Easy, fellas."

Shane pushed Walter's hand away. "This is bullshit!"

Nick's face twisted in a snarl. "You're a freak and a fucking faggot. I can't have that in my office. And you suck at construction because you topple over every time you get hard. Get the fuck out of here. He slammed the door.

Walter said, "Shane, I'm sorry. This is my fault; I shouldn't have talked."

Shane didn't understand. "What did you do? Nick fired me."

Walter nodded. "He's Nick the Dick. He's used to being the big man on the job. Guys used to come here to suck him off, but now that I let your secret slip, they come to see you. His ego is too fragile."

Shane couldn't believe this. There should be laws against this, but no legislator on earth would write the big dick protection bill.

Walter whispered. "I put some extra in there for you to keep you afloat. Nick doesn't even look at the checks. He signed your last paycheck, but he also signed your severance. We don't give severance."

Shane opened the pink envelope. In addition to his paltry pay was a check for $5,000.00. That would pay a few months' rent and nothing else. But it was kind."

"Thanks, Walter. Thank you for owning up to your mistake. I forgive you."

Walter smiled and patted Shane's leg, the one with his dick. "I'll miss seeing this. Sorry I couldn't take it. I hope you find someone who can."

Shane already had.

6

SHACKING UP

Charlie cleared out one of the kids' rooms for Shane. "Stay as long as you want. I'll keep you busy. Just cook me a good dinner, pack my lunch, and keep things clean until you find a good place to land."

Shane was grateful for Charlie's hospitality. He hoped Charlie would open more than just a room to him. He got his wish.

Shane kept the house spotless. He prepared his lunch, cooked his dinner, and then they would settle on the couch for a marathon fucking session every night. Charlie always spent a long time in the bathroom before they got started. Shane wondered what always took so long. He'd soon find out.

Shane got better and better at making Charlie come. Pretty soon, he didn't need his hands at all.

One night, in the throes of passion, Charlie said, "When is it my turn?"

Shane stopped thrusting. "Your turn?"

"To fuck *you*, Shane."

Shane thought about it. "Huh."

"Don't stop; keep fucking! I'm close!"

Shane fucked until they were both fully spent.

Shane said as they lay exhausted on the couch, "I'd like that."

Charlie perked up. "You mean it?"

Shane nodded. "Will it hurt?"

Charlie stroked his chin. "Yeah. It could. But let me break you in."

Shane's thoughts skipped around. Would he like it? Was it painful? How would Charlie 'break him in'? "Tonight?"

Charlie laughed. "I came three times tonight, buddy. Tomorrow, after work. Don't eat lunch."

❧

WHEN CHARLIE GOT HOME THAT NIGHT, SHANE WAS starving. Charlie said, "Let me fix you dinner." He made a chef's salad with oil and vinegar. "It's best if you eat light. You'll see."

Shane's stomach growled even as he ate the rabbit food. He'd noticed Charlie always ate small portions and never thought about it. He was intrigued.

After supper, Shane rose to wash the dishes.

Charlie grabbed his wrist. "Leave them; come with me."

He dragged Shane into the guest bathroom. There was a douche hanging from the shower bar. Charlie took it down and filled it with warm water.

Shane was puzzled. Charlie reassured him. "You won't need much. I'm not gonna go deep, obviously, at least not tonight."

Shane was even more confused. "How can you go deeper?"

Charlie patted his hand. "All in good time. Now lie down on your left side."

Charlie lifted one butt cheek to examine Shane's hole. He whistled. "Christ, that's tight!"

Shane jumped when he felt Charlie's nose between

his cheeks and a tongue at his back door. Charlie licked and pushed until the anus gently gave way, letting him slip in. He spat over and over into the hole.

"Oh fuck that's good." Shane groaned with pleasure. He'd never once had something going in that hole. It felt a lot better than taking a shit.

"Mmmhmm." Charlie's mouth was busy.

Charlie took the thin plastic tip of the douchebag and inserted it. Shane gasped. It was hard but very thin. It didn't hurt, but it felt strange.

Charlie clicked the valve, and water rushed in. Charlie counted to six, then cut off the flow.

Shane started cramping. "Oh, that's weird."

Charlie smiled. "Try to hold it in for a minute."

As Shane waited, the cramps got worse. "I can't."

Charlie gestured. "Go on then!"

Shane said, "Can I have some privacy?"

Charlie stood. "Sure, but it's no big deal if you do it in front of me. It's just business, you know?"

Shane couldn't wait. "Get out!" He rushed to the toilet and sat down as Charlie shut the door. He emptied his bowels. It was unpleasant, but afterward, he felt lighter.

"You done?" Charlie tapped at the door.

"Yeah, come in."

Charlie peered at the water before Shane flushed. "Okay, let's go again."

Shane balked. "Again?"

Charlie nodded. "Don't you want to be clean?"

Shane suddenly got what was happening. This was what kept Charlie busy for so long before they fucked. He was washing out his insides for him. That's what he meant when he said, "I'm not gonna go deep." He probably had to do a deep cleaning every night. That seemed like a lot of work.

He said, "You do this every night for me?"

Charlie nodded. "I like it vanilla. No chocolate."

Shane laughed as Charlie reinserted the tip. "You can stand this time."

Shane didn't wait for Charlie to leave the room; he just sprayed the water into the toilet. Charlie inspected. "Once more, and we're ready."

Charlie had Shane kneel face down on the sofa. He coated a finger with Crisco and pressed in. It hurt. Shane protested for a few seconds, whimpering, then relaxed.

Charlie said, "That's it, baby. Just let it happen." Charlie's finger probed his rectum, palpating his prostate, which made him jump.

"That's the hot button." Charlie pressed it again. "You like that?"

Shane nodded. He wasn't sure he liked it, but it wasn't painful. The more Charlie pressed it, the better it felt.

Charlie took out his finger.

"Now you're ready for this." He pulled out a small butt plug. "This is extra small. It'll only hurt for a split second." He pressed the plug into Shane's hole in a swift motion. Shane gasped, then panted.

Charlie said, "Feels great, right?"

Shane nodded. It did.

Charlie pulled it out, then rammed it back in. Shane groaned.

Charlie said, "I know, right? Best fucking feeling."

After dozens of times, Shane was loose enough not to feel it going in.

Charlie said, "Push it out. I'll catch it." Shane pushed, and the little butt plug shot out, followed by a loud fart. They both laughed.

Charlie said, "You graduated. You're ready for the next size up."

The small looked intimidating. It hurt more and longer than the little one. But after a few dozen cycles, it felt good. Shane liked the full feeling in his ass.

Charlie said, "One more size up, and you're ready for me." The medium butt plug was too big. Shane cried out in agony when Charlie forced it inside. When he pulled it out, he could feel cold air in his ass.

Charlie whistled. "You're a real gaper. I love it." Pop! The plug was back in. It hurt like a motherfucker going in. Charlie went to pull it out.

"Wait! Leave it in for a bit."

Charlie obliged. Shane adjusted to the full feeling. He reached around and wiggled the base, feeling the sides press against his prostate gland. His cock leaked precum. Shane couldn't believe how good it felt, even if it was weird. His ass was not just a hole for food to come out. It was also a sex organ. It opened his eyes to a new world of pleasure.

"You like that, Shane?"

Shane nodded vigorously.

"Good. Then you're ready for me."

Charlie stood. His chunky cock pressed to the upper right against his jeans as he unbuttoned the fly. It leaped out when he tugged on the waistband. When Charlie was impaled on Shane's cock, he was usually only half hard. Shane turned to look and saw that he was much thicker and a little longer than he expected.

Charlie said, "This won't hurt." It did. But not for very long. The warm, slippery flesh against his was an energy circuit. Electrons exchanged between cock and asshole. As Charlie pushed further, Shane's knees wobbled.

"You okay there, right?"

Shane looked over his shoulder and said, "Oh, fuck that feels good."

Charlie winked. "I'm just getting started. Let's do this the right way."

He pulled out and helped Shane flip onto his back, his knees behind his ears. Charlie held the top of his thick cock and leaned in, sliding smoothly into the hole. Shane's cock lolled over his thigh, lifting and pulsing in time to Charlie's thrusts.

"Remember, I made a lot of babies with this. You're in for a real ride. Bisexual men are the best in bed."

Shane grunted. His hole was stretched; his best friend was wedged inside him. It wasn't merely intoxicating; it was addictive. Shane needed more. He pulled Charlie's muscular rump close, burying his friend deep inside. It wasn't enough to pass the junction, but it was extremely satisfying. Each time Charlie pulled back, his nerves relaxed because everything flowed in the expected direction. But going in, his nerves protested. It wasn't pain, though. It was a pleasure unlike any other on Earth. Shane's eyes rolled back into his head as he let his friend have him completely.

When Shane opened his eyes again, he noticed things about Charlie he'd overlooked when he was fucking him. Charlie was far more muscular than Shane. It was the luck of the draw, but he was compact, with bulging biceps and a rippled stomach. With each thrust, the muscles in Charlie's belly contracted, squeezing his navel into a smile. Shane threw his head back onto the cushion, moaning. He'd never felt this good before.

Charlie tapped his shoulder. "Can I cut loose now?"

Shane was puzzled. Charlie was pounding hard in long strokes. What did he mean? It didn't matter. "Yeah, do it."

Like an electric mixer going from low to high, Charlie's strokes shortened, and he moved at a blinding pace. He probably hit ninety strokes a minute. Shane's ass started to twitch, then convulse. He bucked his hips in the throes of an involuntary spasm.

In a high-pitched whine, Shane said, "Oh god, Charlie. Fuck me like a woman."

Beads of sweat poured down Charlie's face as he leaned forward, putting his lips to Shane's. The kiss completed the energy circuit. Cosmic rays flowed between them as they each fell into a whirlpool of sensations.

Shane's cock rose up off his leg. He held it, stroking it gently.

Charlie said, "Oh fuck you're so huge! Oh god! Oh no! I'm gonna come!"

Shane said, "Do it."

Charlie slowed down, then parked his cock all the way inside his friend. He filled Shane with warm liquid in heavy spurts. The energy exchange was so intense that Shane spontaneously shot a load in the air. It landed on Charlie's back.

Charlie collapsed on his friend's chest, kissing his ears, neck, and mouth. Shane felt a sudden need to go to the bathroom. He tried to stand, but Charlie had him pinned down.

"What's wrong?"

Shane said, "I gotta shit."

Charlie laughed. You're clean inside. That's just my swimmers trying to get out.

As Charlie's cock softened, Shane pushed it out, followed by a messy cum flood of biblical proportions.

Charlie saw the damage. "Oh well, I need a new couch anyway."

7
FAROUK

The two friends had become much closer than mere friends or fuck buddies. It was obvious they were in love. Each night when Charlie came home, they took turns in the bathroom, preparing for sex. They crossed that point when a couple begins to dissolve a little. There was bickering. Charlie began to resent how hard he worked, not only to bring in money but to take Shane's impossibly huge cock every night.

Shane didn't have a defense. He was devastated. He worked hard to build a career in construction, and it felt like everything had been taken away from him. He struggled to find another job in the field, but his reputation had spread throughout the industry. He was off balance, and his dick was to blame.

Shane had a secret. As good as he felt with Charlie inside him, he yearned for something more. He often awoke from a dream where his horrible ex-boss plowed him with his cruel cock. He didn't dare tell Charlie about his size fantasies. He knew Charlie had them, of course, or he wouldn't have landed in bed with him. Shane was the ultimate size fantasy come true. But Charlie was the jealous type. If they went grocery shopping together, he watched Shane closely. If Shane caught another man's eye, or even a woman's, Charlie would chew him out on the car ride home.

"Is that how they say, 'Hi' in Whoreville?" Shane had never been in a relationship, and the fighting was unnerving. Shane started to dread the end of the work day.

One night, Charlie came home late. He was drunk.

He said, "Get off the fucking couch and make me some dinner."

Shane obeyed, hoping to avoid a fight. At dinner, Charlie eyed him like a guard dog debating whether a visitor to the property was friend or foe.

"What do you do all fuckin' day while I'm working?"

Shane shrugged. "Clean, mostly. Watch TV. Go through the want ads looking for a job."

Charlie waved a dismissive hand. "Why don't you do something with your fucking hands? I got a whole garage full of tools. Make something!"

It was said with malice, but there was a kernel of an idea in there. Shane smiled. "That's a great idea."

Charlie frowned. "Yeah, it is. What the fuck. You're a genius with your hands." He was starting to sober up, and his disposition became sweeter. "Maybe you can sell some shit."

In the next month, Shane spent his days making things from wood and metal. He was an accomplished welder. Having taken Wood Shop in high school, the techniques all returned to him. He made tables, chairs, and dressers with clamps, glue, buzz-saws, and lathes. He took Polaroids of the pieces and took them around to the mom-and-pop furniture stores looking for a buyer. At Country Barn, he found a lot more than a buyer.

The minute he walked into the store, he knew he'd found the right place. He approached a young girl at the counter.

"May I help you, sir?" She wore her hair in two ponytails like Mary Hartman. She seemed cool.

Shane said, "May I speak to your buyer?"

She tilted her head towards the back of the store. "He's in his office. Go on, I'll let him know you're coming."

A tall, muscular man with olive skin and black hair greeted him at the office door. His green eyes flashed when he saw Shane. They darted downwards, trying to sort out the situation in his pants. Shane didn't care. He adjusted himself to let the guy see what was there.

The man's accent was middle eastern. Maybe Lebanese or Syrian. "I'm Farouk. And you are...?"

He extended a hand. "Shane. Shane Biggars."

"I understand you have some pieces you wish to sell."

Shane got out the small photo album and showed him the pieces.

Farouk was pleased. "These are beautiful. They will work perfectly here. How much for the whole lot?"

Shane was dumbstruck. He hadn't thought this far ahead. Most buyers just said, "Let me think about it, and I'll call you." They never called.

Shane did a tally in his head. Twelve tables, seventy-two chairs, and ten dressers. He'd been busy. He could crank out four chairs per day. Dressers took three days. The tables had a lot of glue time, so they took four days. But he could work on chairs while dressers and tables were drying, which was about a month's worth of full-time work. He took the amount of his monthly paycheck at the construction site and added ten percent. "I'll take $2,200.00 for the whole lot."

Farouk whistled. "In my country, the seller starts ridiculously high, and the buyer returns with a ridiculously low price."

Shane thought maybe he'd gone too high. It was the opposite.

Farouk said, "I will give you $5,000.00, but it's worth much more. I won't expect such a reasonable price the next time you come."

Shane was astonished. He'd never imagined his work was worth so much. Farouk could see the wonder in his eyes. They shook hands, and Farouk wrote him a check. Shane pocketed the money.

Farouk's eyes darted downwards again. "Now that business is done, let's discuss pleasure."

Shane felt a tingling. Farouk's desire was in the air. Men give off a scent when they want sex. It's their animal nature.

Farouk said, "I imagine with such a big prize, you rarely find a partner."

Shane shrugged. "I got one."

Farouk cleared his throat, flexing his biceps and pectoral muscles as he stroked his chin. "One is not nearly enough."

Shane said, "I doubt you could handle this." He squeezed the base of his cock and lifted it, revealing the full length below his knee.

Farouk laughed. "I don't want that. I want this." He put his hand on Shane's bottom. "But I fear you can't handle me."

This was an answer to Shane's prayer. He was taken by surprise. Was Farouk bigger than Charlie? He said, "Show me."

Farouk locked the door to his office. He squeezed his trouser leg, revealing the outline of a long, snake-like cock that ended with a massive head. It dwarfed Charlie's cock by a mile. "Do you want to try?"

Shane's guilt evaporated in a pool of hot lust. He nodded.

Farouk lowered his pants, revealing a long, thick, brown cock with a pink head. It was still soft but growing. It lifted away from his legs, pointing at a downward 45-degree angle. Farouk removed a tube of ointment from his desk drawer and applied it liberally to his cock. He worked a finger inside Shane's hole. It smelled of roses and cardamom.

The swarthy shop owner asked, "Are you ready to go to heaven?"

Shane bent forward in response, pulling his ass cheeks apart. Farouk held his waist with one hand, his cock head with the other. He guided it to Shane's hole and pressed.

Shane felt the colossal head pushing against his hole but couldn't relax enough to let it in. Farouk slapped his ass hard, pushing at the same time. The momentary astonishment allowed him entry. It hurt.

Farouk said, "Don't worry. I'm an expert. You won't feel any pain once we get past this." With the tip of his cock wedged inside Shane, he let go and pulled Shane closer with both hands. The cock head wasn't flared; it was cylindrical. Once the widest part was in, it flowed smoothly into his ass. Shane saw stars.

"Ow! Fuck!"

Farouk said, "Shh! Annabelle will hear us. Bite this." He put a wood sample in Shane's mouth. Biting down helped. It was a soft wood, like a pencil, and it yielded to his teeth. He feared he would end up with a mouth full of sawdust if it kept hurting so much. But then, just as Farouk had promised, it stopped hurting.

"Better, right?"

Shane nodded. It felt great. With an expert's technique, Farouk pushed smoothly to the back of Shane's rectum, filling it and stretching it wider than Charlie ever had. His strong hands twisted Shane at the waist, allowing him passage to the sacred inner sanctum: the colon. Shane thought it would hurt, but it didn't. It was a sudden pop, like a handclap, and the cock slid into new territory. The nerves in the sigmoid colon were much more sensitive. Shane shivered.

Farouk leaned forward and whispered. "Are you in heaven yet?"

Shane nodded.

Farouk laughed. "No, this is purgatory. Just wait." He pulled Shane close gracefully until he was lodged deep in his colon. Shane's butt cheeks squished into Farouk's thighs.

Farouk shuddered. "Oh, it's been too long. I'm close already."

Shane didn't care. This was the fuck he'd dreamed of, only bigger. Farouk rocked his hips up and down, sliding back and forth in Shane's tight hole.

"You are so handsome! Even from behind!" The shop owner caressed Shane's face. He lifted Shane, rotating him, so he sat on the desk sideways, Farouk still entering him from behind but with a better view.

Shane wished Farouk would go faster, but then it wouldn't last. He plunged in and out of the second hole in slow, rhythmic strokes, each time making a soft clapping sound. Charlie's bunny-fucking was so different from this slow, firm invasion. Farouk closed his eyes. "I can't believe how huge you are. Will you come for me? I need to know I made that big dick come."

Shane took his heavy meat in his hands and stroked it rapidly. Farouk put a hand over Shane's. "Slowly. Savor it."

That was the theme of this fuck. Slow and steady. It was different. It began to grow on Shane. Sex wasn't always just a race to get off. It could be a glorious road trip to nirvana.

Shane swung a leg over to fully face Farouk. He looked into his eyes, connecting, feeling what he was feeling, and breathing in time. The contours of his face were graceful, but his salt-and-pepper stubble and rough body skin were a masculine contrast. He had beauty and brawn in equal measure. Shane locked his ankles behind Farouk's midsection and pulled him closer.

"Deeper, eh?"

Shane nodded. Farouk planted his hands on Shane's chest, pushing him back onto the desk. He lifted his ankles to his shoulders, then leaned forward until Shane's legs bent, dangling down Farouk's back. Farouk pushed harder and harder until his pubic mound ground into Shane's asshole. It hit a nerve, and Shane had a whole different kind of orgasm. Charlie could never give him this. His tummy twitched, and his hips bucked. He was in ecstasy. He lay back, looking at the Celotex ceiling, absently counting the holes in a single square. The fluorescent light buzz was the only sound besides the soft, gentle clapping sounds of Farouk's cock moving in and out.

Farouk said, "I'm here. Are you close?"

The words were like magic. Shane felt a tingling in his balls.

The owner said, "Same time. You nod when it's time."

Shane continued the slow, long rubs up and down his cock. His balls contracted. Shane nodded.

Farouk pushed in, up to the limit, and unleashed a flood of hot Middle-Eastern sperm in Shane's belly. At the same time, Shane's cock became an obelisk fountain, spraying the room with his essence.

Farouk pulled out suddenly, leaving a gaping hole in Shane's backside. The sudden emptiness caused him to cramp. He doubled over, writhing in a paroxysm of pleasure. Farouk grinned. "My special trick."

As Shane buttoned his pants and tightened his belt, Farouk wrote down a number.

He said, "I need a favor. Will you please teach Nasir, my son? You need an apprentice because my next order is much bigger, anyway."

❧ 8 ❧

NASIR

That night, Charlie came home in a good mood. "I got a raise. Nick the Dick came through for me!"

Shane kissed his lover. "That's wonderful news, hon. I sold my furniture, too."

"How many pieces?"

"All of them. For five thousand dollars."

Nick sat down hard on the couch. "That's fuckin' great!"

That night, when they made love, Charlie said, "I smell roses and spice. What is that?"

Shane shrugged. "It must be the hand soap at Farouk's place. It smelled nice." He didn't like lying but also didn't think Charlie would like the truth.

In the morning, after Charlie left, Shane called Nasir. The boy came over, dragging his heels. He avoided Shane's gaze, watching his shoes like they were a tennis match. This was going to be a challenge.

He led the boy to the garage, showing him the different equipment. Nasir gradually warmed up to Shane. He helped position the planks for a table, clamping them together with wood glue. While that was drying, they worked on some chairs. The wood turner was probably one of the safest tools in the shop, so he tasked Nasir with turning spindles and legs for the chairs. The boy was a natural. By noon, he'd turned enough wood for a dozen chairs.

"How old are you, Nasir?"

"Twenty-three." Shane was surprised he was the same age as him.

"You look much younger."

Nasir said, "I shave my beard. I look like my Dad if I let it grow in."

Nasir didn't have the thick accent of his father. He spoke like a surfer dude. His skin was darker than his father's, probably from spending a lot of time at the beach.

"Do you surf?" Shane was curious.

"I boogie board. I can't stand on a surfboard. I lose my balance too easily."

Shane laughed. "I got fired at my old job for losing my balance."

Nasir sighed. Under his breath, he said, "Probably not for the same reason."

Shane nodded in agreement. "Yeah, my reason is pretty bizarre."

Nasir looked up from the lathe. "What do you mean?"

Shane wasn't sure the conversation was appropriate work talk. He looked away. "It's a physical problem."

Nasir said, "Me, too." Then his eyes darted down below Shane's waistline. They saw nothing, of course, because Shane's baggy pants revealed nothing.

Shane couldn't help himself. He stole a glance at Nasir's crotch. He wore the same type of baggy trousers. There was a long silence.

Nasir said, "Maybe we have the same problem." He softly touched his leg. It spoke volumes to Shane but wouldn't have meant anything to someone without his problem.

Shane held the base of his cock and tugged, revealing the python in his pants.

Nasir took a step back. "Holy shit, dude. You got me beat by a mile!"

After more awkward moments passed, Shane returned to the buzz saw, cutting dovetails in the wood for the dresser drawer. Nasir watched him, learning.

Shane tried to take his mind off Nasir and his big dick, but it was screaming like an echo in his head.

Finally, Shane said, "I'll show you mine if you show me yours."

Nasir frowned. "That's kinda gay, dude."

Shane shrugged. "No problem. It's not a command, just an offer."

Nasir licked his lips. "Okay. I wanna see it. It can't be as big as it looks in your pants."

Shane extracted his enormous soft cock from his pants, letting it flop over the waistband and dangle to his knees.

Nasir nearly fainted. He took two steps backward and sat on a sawhorse. "Shit, dude. Seeing that makes me want to try surfing after all."

Shane put a hand on his hip. "Let's see what you're working with."

Nasir sheepishly pulled out what would be a gigantic soft cock in any other situation. It was thick as his wrist and hung to his mid-thigh. He said, "Mine doesn't grow. Does yours?"

Shane nodded. "Yeah, a lot."

Nasir wiped the sweat from his brow. "I'm pretty lonely. It must be worse for you."

"I found someone," Shane said, "So I'm pretty lucky. What about you?"

Nasir said, "I can date Muslim girls because they don't want sex before marriage. But California girls are horn dogs. And when they see this," he gestured to his fat cock, "they head for the hills."

The two men stood facing one another, gazing at the other's cock. Nasir started to get hard. He averted his eyes, trying to put it away, but it wouldn't fit back through the opening of his waist. Powerless over his cock, Nasir watched it lift, swelling only slightly.

Shane smiled. "Nothing to be embarrassed about." His was stretching and swelling at the sight of the young man's heavy endowment, even bigger than his father's.

Nasir said, "Fuck! This fucking thing is so embarrassing!"

Shane frowned. "Hey, be proud of your difference. It's going to make someone very happy someday. Mine does."

Nasir threw his hands up. "Who's the lucky lady? Is she ten feet tall? I mean fuck, that's huge."

Shane hesitated. "He's actually a little shorter than me."

"I knew it! A fucking fag!" Nasir ran out of the garage.

Shane unbuttoned his pants, tucking his softening cock back down his leg. He waited to hear the front door slam and Nasir's car start, but it didn't happen. After about ten minutes, Nasir poked his head into the workshop.

"Uh, look, dude. I was out of line. My dad's gay. I know better.

Shane smiled. "It's cool, Nasir. It took me a while to be comfortable with it, too. It's not easy."

Nasir went back to the lathe, turning spindles to calm down. A half dozen times, he started to ask a question, then stopped. At last, he came out with it.

"Did my Dad...you know...do it with you?"

Shane nodded. "It felt great."

Nasir gestured towards the house. "How does he feel about it?"

Shane said, "He doesn't know."

Nasir worked in silence. At last, he said, "I'm a virgin. I've never fucked anybody." He unconsciously rubbed his leg, stroking his cock.

Shane watched the boy grapple with his emotions. "I was, too, until recently."

Nasir said, "How did you know you were gay?"

"I didn't. I wasn't sexual at all until my boss and my assistant changed that. Then Charlie came along, and it was love. I wasn't gay or straight before that. My dick was just too damn big, and I had given up on all of it."

Nasir turned off the lathe. "I don't want to be gay like my dad."

Shane said, "Then don't be."

Nasir swallowed. "I mean, I don't WANT to be." His eyes were smoldering as he looked Shane up and down. "I don't want to be like him."

Shane took a chance. "Then be gay like you, not him."

Wordlessly, Nasir lowered his pants. He held his cock and stroked it, looking at Shane. "Can you take it?"

Shane nodded. "I can, and I want to."

Nasir said, "I don't know what to do. Will you show me?"

Shane pulled out a bottle of sweet almond oil. He squeezed a line on Nasir's throbbing cock, and coated it. He put the nozzle inside the opening of his ass and gave a quick squeeze, soaking his insides.

He lay on the sawhorse, his legs in the air. Nasir stepped forward, and Shane rested his legs on Nasir's shoulders. He held the cock in his hand and guided it to his hole. Nasir was in a hurry. He pushed too hard, and Shane's hole tightened.

"Easy, Nasir. Just press gently.'

Nasir tried again. This time, the tip found its way past the tight ring. Shane tugged, forcing more of the thick flesh into his bottom. Like his father, Nasir's head was a cylinder. Once it crowned, it slid in smoothly.

Nasir moaned. "Fu-u-u-ck, that's good."

Shane repeated the move he'd made with the father. He hooked his ankles just above Nasir's ass and pulled him closer. The cock reached the end of the rectum.

"Shit. I knew it." Nasir was disappointed. He was only halfway in. Shane twisted, letting him slide into the colon. Nasir's eyes widened.

"Shit, did I poke a hole in you, dude?"

Shane laughed. "No. Keep going."

Nasir stepped into it, pushing hard until his massive cock was tightly wedged deep inside Shane.

The young man said, "No kissing. Just fucking."

Shane was cool with all of it. Nasir was the biggest he'd ever had. Kissing might have made it easier, but he was high on the sensation of being completely filled. This must be that high that Charlie had chased so hard that it scared his wife and kids away. It was like a drug, for sure.

"Oh, shit, I'm gonna come!"

Nasir had a hair trigger. It was his first time; of course, it was quick. Deep inside, Shane felt a volley of warm spurts in his guts. Nasir shook, his mouth in an "O," and his eyes closed. His cock began to soften. It didn't shrink.

Shane didn't have time to come. He hadn't even started to play with himself.

Nasir picked up the semi-hard cock dangling off of Shane's left leg and put the tip of the head in his mouth. He licked it, slurping the huge urethra like it was a pussy. Shane was astonished. No one, not even Charlie, had attempted this with him. Nasir would need to be a boa constrictor to open his jaws wide enough, but he sucked on the tip like a nursing baby. As Nasir's mouth grew more passionate, Shane felt a stiffening inside his guts. The boy was hard again. He sucked the head of the gargantuan cock, fucking Shane's ass at the same time.

Shane liked being sucked, even if it wasn't anything like a full blow job. It caused him to swell thicker, making his cock heavy. Nasir held it with both hands, jerking it up and down.

Shane's balls tingled. This boy was good. "Nasir, I'm gonna come."

Nasir nodded but never ceased sucking, swirling his tongue in and around the piss-hole. He jerked Shane harder.

"Nasir, oh shit! I'm gonna come! I'm coming!"

Nasir caught the whole load in his mouth. At the same time, he came again. Nasir couldn't swallow fast enough. Cum blasted past his lips, spraying both men with Shane's load.

Shane unlocked his ankles, allowing Nasir to withdraw inch after inch of sticky, slick cock, until the head popped out, slapping the boy's thigh. There was so much cum in Shane's guts that he started to cramp. A trickle came out, followed by a glob, then Shane's guts contracted, blowing a giant load of cum on the floor.

Nasir grabbed a shop towel, wiping his cock, then Shane's bum and chest, which were sticky with both men's juices.

Shane cracked a smile. "So yeah, you're hired!"

They both laughed.

9

SHANE, CHARLIE, AND NASIR

All month, Shane and Nasir built furniture for six hours, then fucked for two. Nasir's technique improved. He learned how to jackrabbit like Charlie and how to fuck slowly like his father. There was nearly twice as much inventory at month's end. Nasir helped his father load up the truck to haul off the furniture. Charlie came home, seeing Nasir for the first time.

Nasir smiled and extended a hand. "Hi, Nasir."

Charlie looked him up and down. He had to suppress a wolf whistle. "Charlie. I'm Shane's boyfriend."

"I know."

Farouk came around the side of the truck and introduced himself. "Your boyfriend is a good teacher. My son is learning so much from him." If only he knew how true that was!

Charlie nodded. He watched Shane and Nasir exchange glances. "I'll bet he is."

Farouk left a check for 7,500.00 dollars. Charlie couldn't believe it. Shane had made three months' salary in one month. Of course, Shane had to pay Nasir $1,500.00, but it was still a tremendous amount of money. Enough to buy a small truck if they needed one. They didn't.

After Nasir hopped in his Camaro and took off, Charlie took Shane by the wrist. "You're the big daddy today."

Shane punished Charlie's ass that night. He jackrabbited, slow-fucked, and pounded him senseless. Charlie moaned, shooting his load with no hands twice. Shane filled him to overflowing. They fell asleep in each other's arms.

In the morning, Charlie made bacon and eggs. Shane wiped the sleep out of his eyes and sat at the breakfast table.

Charlie put a plate in front of him. "We should talk about Nasir."

Shane's mouth went dry. "What about?"

"I want to fuck his ass, that's what."

Shane nearly choked on his bacon. "I don't think he'd like that."

Charlie laughed. "I know how to make him like it. If he likes fucking your ass so much, he'll like a normal cock like mine up his butt."

The word 'normal' stung a bit. "What makes you think Nasir is fucking me?"

Charlie said, "Your ass smells like Almond Oil every night. I find little jelly babies up there. If it's not Nasir, then someone is fucking you in there."

Charlie had caught him red-handed and almond-assed. He didn't try to lie any further. "Yeah, you got me."

Charlie was excited. "So you'll talk to him about it?"

Shane nodded. "I can ask. I doubt he'll agree to it."

❧

IT TURNED OUT SHANE WAS WRONG. NASIR WAS attracted to Charlie with his short body and thick muscles. "Your boyfriend is fucking hot. He's into me? He'll let me fuck him?"

Shane was halfway to the truth. "Yeah, he'll fuck you."

Nasir gave a quizzical look. "Wait, he wants to fuck me?"

Shane nodded.

"Won't it hurt?"

Shane shrugged. "I was a virgin. Charlie was my first. He's got a whole technique."

Nasir pounded a fist into his palm. "Damn, I always wanted to try it. There's no way I would let you do that to me. How big is Charlie?"

"Big enough." Shane held up two fingers, holding them about six inches apart. He made a circle with his thumb and forefinger, about five inches around.

Nasir clapped his hands, bouncing on his feet. "Oh fuck, this is so cool! Can I fuck you while he fucks me?"

Shane smiled. "You can do whatever you want."

That night, when Charlie came home, Nasir and Shane sat on the couch, drinking beers and watching the evening news.

Charlie tilted his head at Shane. "Is he?"

Shane nodded. "It's a go."

Charlie led Nasir into the bathroom for a thorough cleaning. When Shane passed the open door, he saw Charlie stroking Nasir's cock. It was a really nice one. Huge when not sitting side by side with Shane's monster. Charlie looked overjoyed.

The three men arranged themselves in bed. Charlie started by putting the extra-small butt plug in Nasir's hole. Nasir wriggled. "More."

He was looser than Shane had been. He had graduated to the medium butt plug in just twenty minutes.

Charlie sat on the edge of the bed, his stiff cock throbbing against his navel. Nasir straddled him, sitting slowly. Charlie leaned back, allowing Nasir to slide downwards. Shane watched with envy as his boyfriend easily penetrated the beautiful boy.

"Fuck! Oh, fuck that feels good!" Nasir closed his eyes, savoring each throb of Charlie's perfect-sized cock. Nasir rode Charlie for a minute or two, then lay in the middle of the bed, legs in the air. Charlie scooped up his legs and skillfully penetrated the eager apprentice.

Shane felt left out. He came around behind Charlie, stroking his cock, and pushed his way inside his boyfriend. It was a little awkward, but there was so much cock for Shane to work with that it didn't take long till he was fucking his boyfriend hard. Charlie moaned, softening inside Nasir, who struggled to keep Charlie inside him. Shane had to pull out. They rearranged, so Charlie was fucking Nasir doggy style, and Nasir fucked Shane. That worked. Nasir was so excited he kept his hard-on even with Charlie pushing on his ass. Shane stared up into Nasir's eyes. The boy was the "lucky Pierre," pinned between the two lovers, plugging one hole while getting stuffed himself.

Nasir moaned softly. "Oh man, this is so fucking great. I mean, it's weird, but it's great."

Shane thought it was a little weird, too, but anything that felt this good could be as strange as it needed to be.

Nasir was deep in Shane's colon, dragging his baby-maker back and forth in rhythmic strokes. When Charlie started pounding hard and fast, it passed through Nasir into Shane. The powerful vibrations reverberated through all three men. There was a collective moan; it sounded like a room full of dying soldiers. Pleasure had reached its peak.

Charlie was first. "Oh god, oh shit, Nasir, here it comes."

Nasir threw his head from side to side, thrashing. "Come inside me, man."

Charlie obliged. The two men moaned collectively.

Charlie collapsed on Nasir's back. The strong youngster continued to pound Shane's hole. Their eyes locked.

In an invisible language, the two men instinctively brought their lips together. Nasir never kissed Shane, but now that he was full of Charlie's cum, a veil had lifted. They kissed passionately until Nasir pulled back. "Oh man, I'm gonna come."

Shane put a hand behind his neck and pulled him close. As Nasir painted Shane's insides with his thick cum, they kissed. Nasir pulled out slowly, leaving his cum deep inside Shane.

Charlie lifted Shane's hard cock and sat on it. Nasir watched in amazement as Charlie sat down until his ass was in Shane's lap. Shane bucked and thrust upward, holding Charlie's ass aloft to allow for better thrusts.

Then Nasir saw the outline of Shane's cock against Charlie's tight tummy. He took his hardening cock in hand and jacked off, watching Charlie getting filled and stretched beyond all belief.

"Oh fuck, that's hot!"

Charlie smiled. "You're next. Save it."

Nasir's jaw went slack. "I can't take that thing."

Charlie laughed. "No, I meant I'll take you for a pony ride next. Just save that load for me."

Shane was excited by the new energy in the room. He didn't even have time to warn Charlie when his balls tingled. His load came out suddenly, in bursts. Charlie held his hands to his guts, squeezing the massive firehose cock as it filled him with goopy cum. He stood up, cum dripping from the gaping hole, and sat down on Nasir's hard cock. It was Charlie's turn to kiss Nasir. Shane watched, a little bored, while his boyfriend and Nasir bonded. It wasn't long before the young lad had left his load inside the other lover.

Exhausted, the three men fell asleep in each other's arms.

10

MIDTOWNE

S hane's business was brisk. He had an exclusive with Farouk, which made both men very rich. Nasir went from intern to apprentice to employee. It was nothing like the construction work that Shane had trained for, but it was far more satisfying in every way, including Nasir's frequent visits to his ass. But as time wore on, they became less frequent.

Shane was grateful for Nasir, but his jealousy increased each time Charlie fucked him. Charlie was cool with the three-way arrangement, but he got the best of all worlds. He fucked everyone and got fucked by everyone in four glorious pairs. Nasir and Shane were limited to three pairings. It was just stupid math, but it pissed Shane off. He watched while he and his lover drifted apart. Increasingly, Nasir and Charlie spent more of the night together, trying new things, leaving Shane out of the equation. He was hurt, lonely, and depressed.

Farouk saw Shane's sadness and commented.

"I see you sad, my friend. What's wrong?"

Shane sighed. "Don't get me wrong, I'm crazy about your son, but he and Charlie are shutting me out."

Farouk put an arm around Shane. "You are my son, too. I know you have no Father, and I want you to rely on me. I'm your gay daddy." He chuckled. "If you're un-happy, why don't you leave?"

Shane put his head in his hands. "I won't ever find anyone else like Charlie. He's the only one who can take me. And he only does it like every third day now. Nasir gets first dibs."

Farouk held Shane. "Hey, you must know that Charlie isn't the only person in the world who has trained for a man like you."

Shane looked up. "Do you know anyone else?"

Farouk shook his head. "No, but I haven't looked around much. My wife was extraordinary, but she hated sex with me. Once Nasir was born, she put her foot down. Nothing would go up there ever again."

Shane looked into Farouk's eyes and saw sadness there.

"So I found men, a few men, who not only could take it but even loved it. I didn't want a relationship."

Shane wondered if this handsome man was telling the truth. Don't most people yearn to be with some-one? Even in his many years of celibacy, Shane had longed to be close with another person. The love he'd found with Charlie was slipping away, and it hurt.

Shane said, "Where did you find men?"

Farouk smiled. "There are many places to meet men. I recommend a bathhouse because your whole package will be displayed before you begin anything. It saves time for big men like you and me."

"What's a bathhouse?"

Farouk put a fatherly arm around Shane's shoulders. "My son, I will show you."

❧

THE MIDTOWNE SPA WAS A FOUR-STORY BUILDING ON the eastern edge of downtown Los Angeles. Farouk drove his Cadillac, paying extra for valet parking. The sign at the ticket booth advertised a lunchtime special. For six dollars each, Shane and Farouk got a towel and the key to a locker.

"If it is a weekend, I'll get a room," Farouk said. "But for lunchtime, it's a waste of money."

The two men undressed, earning gasps of surprise from nearby bath patrons. Shane hitched the towel around his waist and followed Farouk to the ground floor, which featured a pool, dry sauna, steam room, and whirlpool.

The two men soaked in the hot whirlpool, their cocks floating to the surface with the bubbles. In twos and threes, men walked by, whispering. The hairs on Shane's neck went stiff. He felt like a zoo animal, the way men pointed and stared.

A blond-haired, blue-eyed elf of a boy joined them in the hot tub. He eyed both men greedily.

The silence seemed awkward. Shane said, "I'm Shane; what's your name?" He extended a hand.

The boy giggled. "Is this your first time at a bathhouse?"

Shane was hurt. "Yeah. Why?"

The boy smiled broadly. "Oh my god! A virgin!"

Farouk leaned to whisper in Shane's ear. "We keep it anonymous here. I should have told you that. I'm sorry."

The boy looked from one man to another. He said, "I'm a size queen, but that," he indicated Shane's colossal log, "is too big for me. Now you, on the other hand, are a perfect fit."

He put a hand on Farouk's fat cock head and squeezed."

So far, this wasn't working out very well. Shane was miffed.

"I'm gonna catch a cab home. This is a waste of time."

Farouk put a calming hand on Shane's shoulder. "Be

patient. Speak with your eyes, not your mouth. Go for a walk and explore the other floors. I'll meet you here in thirty minutes."

The boy with blue eyes took Farouk's hand and led him upstairs. Shane started to feel dizzy. He exited the hot tub and jumped in the much cooler pool. It felt good. He swam naked for the first time. He could feel his cock dragging beneath him, hitting his thighs and knees as it rippled through the water. Swimming relaxed him. He did ten or twelve laps before stopping in the shallow end. He was out of breath, and it felt great.

At the other corner of the shallow end, a man with short auburn hair, freckles, and a mustache eyed him hungrily. He swam to Shane's corner and leaned against the tiles beside him.

The redhead said softly, "I've got a room. What are you into?"

Shane wasn't sure how to answer. "Uh, fucking."

The man had a pleasant smile. "Getting fucked or fucking?"

Shane shrugged. "Both."

"Come on." The freckled man got out of the water, leading Shane by his hand. Shane grabbed his towel, throwing it over one shoulder, letting his massive cock swing like a baby elephant trunk as he marched to the man's room. He resisted asking the man's name, occupation, birth sign, or making any other nervous small talk. He stole a few glances at the man's soft cock, which was smaller than he expected.

The room was bleak. There was a thin foam mattress, a table lamp, and little else. The walls were painted black. When the man closed the door, they were in near darkness.

Wordlessly, the man gestured until Shane was lying on his back, legs in the air. The man grabbed hold of Shane's thick cock, using it to steady himself as he navigated his way to Shane's hole.

The man's cock was filling with blood now. It rose off the mattress, stretching rapidly until it was three times as long and twice as fat. It was a bludgeon of a cock, nearly as big as Farouk's.

The man said, "I'm a grower, not a shower."

Shane said, "Okay. Show me."

The man buried his nose between Shane's ass cheeks, hungrily licking his hole. Shane was tense at first, but the man's tongue was a sedative. He relaxed, letting his sphincter unclench.

"Nice!" The man praised Shane, then dug deeper into his hole.

Shane came down out of his head. He was in the moment, just enjoying being sexual with a handsome stranger. He rubbed the man's head, enjoying the coarse carpet of hair. The man kept licking and prodding until Shane was loose.

"Here." The man handed him a bottle of amyl nitrite. "You know how it works?"

Shane shook his head. The man took the bottle back, covered a nostril, and inhaled. He handed it back to Shane and motioned him to follow his example.

Shane inhaled the chemical brew, which reminded him of building plastic models as a kid. Suddenly, the dark room was bright red. His head lolled back, and he forgot he had a body. The redhead was lodged deep inside him when the feeling wore off, knocking on the second doorway.

"You've got a huge fucking dick." The man looked into Shane's eyes as he fucked him. "I'll bet nobody lets you fuck them, am I right?"

Shane disliked the question. He shook his head rather than give the man the satisfaction of a clear answer. When the man opened his mouth to ask another question, Shane put a finger over the guy's lips.

"Shh. Don't speak."

In this way, they fucked silently. Shane tuned into

the rhythm of the man's thrusts, meeting them with his own force. Their energies combined and mingled as the energy of pure sex fueled their lust. The man was just long enough to play peek-a-boo with the second hole. The feeling was both intoxicating and frustrating in equal measure. If Shane was going to get fucked, he wanted to be completely filled. This man was far bigger than most, but he wasn't quite in that particular class like Nasir or Farouk. He was an inch too short and needed another inch of girth to fill Shane's glass to the top. It left him wanting. He was half hard, certain he wouldn't come with this man. But he wanted the man to come inside him.

"I'm close, man. Are you gonna join me?"

Shane shook his head. He said, "Do it. Come inside me."

The man picked up the pace. "Oh shit, here it comes!"

Like any sexual encounter, the moment where a man spills his seed inside Shane felt magical. He held the man's pulsing, heavy balls as they emptied inside him. When it was over, the man stood and gestured for the door. Wordlessly, Shane left the room, a trickle of cum running down his leg.

In the nearby shower, Shane washed his bottom. There was a shallow, empty spot in his heart. As thrilling as the wordless sex had been, it wasn't a connection. His connection with his dear friend Charlie was fading, and he didn't want to feel this alone. As he soaped up his cock and balls, he heard gasps of astonishment from nearby shower heads. He ignored them, lost in thought. He looked up and saw that he was ten minutes late to meet Farouk. He took the stairs two at a time, not bothering to dry off. Farouk was waiting in the whirlpool.

"How was it?"

Shane shrugged. "I met a guy; we fucked."

Farouk laughed hard. "That is the shortest, most complete answer to that question I could have imagined."

Shane smiled. "And you?"

Farouk gestured to his soft cock floating at the water's surface. "He was in over his head, but he persevered. I taught him some new tricks."

Shane enjoyed bonding with this older man over dick size. He was like a father in many ways, he imagined, never having known his own father. He imagined that most fathers didn't take their sons to gay bathhouses, but in this case, it seemed like an appropriate, fatherly thing to do.

The clock showed 2pm. The bathhouse emptied out. Businessmen, shop clerks, and laborers returned to their jobs. Lunch was over.

"Does it always empty out like this?"

Farouk nodded. "During the week. On Friday, Saturday, and Sunday, this place stays busy 24 hours."

Shane said, "I think I'll return on the weekend."

❧ 11 ❧

HOGAN

On Saturday, Nasir and Charlie had plans to go see the Dodgers. They hadn't bought Shane a ticket. He wasn't a big baseball fan, anyway. He was excited to be the odd man out because it meant he could go to the Midtowne Spa without any explanation to his two lovers. As he climbed in his truck, he got a boner. He couldn't wait to see the place again.

He got a room this time, even though it cost twenty dollars. Saturday was a much more crowded day. There were men of every shape, size, color, and creed. There were short men with dicks so big they looked like they would topple over. There were tall men with little nubs for a penis, like Walter's. He saw Walter on the third floor, giving a blow job to an attractive older man, but Walter didn't see Shane.

He found that wearing a towel was a better idea than walking around advertising his humongous cock. It didn't entirely hide the tip, which swung below the knee line. He saw a man with a longer towel.

"Where did you get that?"

The man looked down and grinned. "I see you have an even bigger problem than I do. Just ask at the front desk. They don't ask questions, usually."

Walter turned in the small towel in exchange for a much bigger one covering his shins.

With all that nonsense out of the way, Walter found his room, closed the door, and relaxed in the dark. He nodded off to sleep.

His watch said he slept for about an hour. He cursed himself for wasting time while he was on the clock. The room was only good for eight hours. He wanted to get in as much fucking as humanly possible. He hoped he would find a cock-hungry bottom with an elastic hole. If there were any place in Los Angeles to find one, it would be here.

He started on the roof and planned to work his way down. On Monday, the roof had just been a place to smoke cigarettes. Saturdays, the roof was an orgy. With the skyline of downtown looming over them, the men were in groups of three, four, or more, doing every kind of kinky sex act Shane had ever imagined. There were fists, whips, chains, handcuffs...it was overwhelming.

He turned sharply to walk away, and his towel fell. There was an audible collective gasp as every eye on the roof locked onto his dick.

An older gentleman in a leather jockstrap waved him over. His arm was halfway up a little guy's bum. The guy, kneeling on a chaise lounge, might have been high on drugs. His eyes fluttered, and he moaned like a waterfront whore.

"Here. You take over...with that." The leather man pointed to Shane's hardening cock. "Hogan can take it."

A large crowd gathered to watch as Shane, feeling embarrassed, pushed his way easily into the loose, sloppy hole.

Hogan squealed with delight. "Oh, Jesus fucking Christ, you're huge! Oh, God. Oh, Mary!"

Shane was a little turned off by the guy's babbling. He felt a cruel, dark master take him over. "Shut up when I'm fucking you."

The man clamped his mouth shut, barely able to contain the cries of pain behind his sealed lips.

Each time Shane thrust, the chaise lounge bumped forward. Shane grabbed the chair with one hand and put his other arm around the little guy's neck. This allowed him to break past the second hole. The guy let out a blood-curdling shriek. Shane stopped. Had he gone too far?"

Hogan whispered, "Please, sir, don't stop."

Shane bore down hard, forcing his hips forward until they rested on the man's round butt cheeks. His cock pushed outward from behind the man's navel, forming a huge lump. A series of gasps and even faint applause erupted at this sight.

Shane whispered in the little man's ear. "You ready for this?"

"Yes, Daddy. Fuck me hard."

Shane went to town. He didn't know anyone and didn't care. He was a prize bull in a vast arena, and the little guy was his matador for him to trample. He fucked so hard and deep that he imagined his cock would pop out of the guy's mouth! This made him harder, which stretched the walls of the little man's innards. The boy shrieked, clamping his hand over his mouth to stifle the scream.

Shane leaned in. "Am I hurting you?"

The guy nodded.

"You want me to stop?"

He shook his head vigorously. Shane tore through the man's innards, reaching the descending colon. The man went into a spasm, twitching violently. Every cock on the roof was hard. Men jacked off in astonishment while watching the extraordinary sex show.

Shane went into high gear like Charlie had taught him. His butt was a blur as he pounded in and out of the boy's colon. He felt a tingling in his balls; it was time.

"You want me to come in you?"

Hogan didn't even nod. He was somewhere else, eyes glazed and mouth whispering nonsense syllables.

"Oh fuck! Here it comes! Take it!" Shane shot a massive load inside the boy.

When he let go, the boy collapsed forward onto the chaise lounge, unconscious.

The crowd murmured. "Somebody call an ambulance. Hogan's hurt again."

Indeed, when Shane pulled out, the boy's ass bled profusely. He saw thick chunks of his cum mingled with the blood, dying it pink.

The crowd dispersed. Only good Samaritans remained, tending the boy with towels and a glass of water.

"If I die, I will die happy." Hogan turned and looked at Shane over his shoulder. He cracked a smile before fainting again.

The ambulance arrived, hauling off the kid. The last of the onlookers left, leaving Shane with the emergency workers. Shane was grateful his towel stayed around his waist this time.

A dark-haired, handsome cop approached Shane. "I need to ask you a few questions."

Shane nodded.

"How did this young man get injured so badly?"

Shane looked away, unsure how to answer. He tried. "It was, uh, I was too big for him."

The cop frowned. "Too big?"

Shane patted the front of his towel, embarrassed to say more.

The cop showed his teeth when he smiled. "Me, too."

Shane's eyes drifted below the cop's holster; he spied a thick bulge running down one leg.

The cop leaned in. "Between you and me, I know

that little bitch. Hogan always bites off more than he can chew. He's insatiable."

Shane wasn't expecting such brazen language from a cop.

A second police officer ambled over. "What's the story, Rocco?"

Rocco patted his mustache. "Our friend here - what's your name?"

"Shane"

"Shane has the same problem I do."

The other cop's eyes went immediately below Shane's waist. "He can't be like you, Rocco."

Rocco shrugged. "Probably not, Ashe. He'd have to show us." He turned to Shane. "You don't want to show us, do you?"

The way Rocco's eyes twinkled caused a stirring in Shane's loins. He felt his cock lifting off his leg involuntarily. The cop named Ashe took a big step back. "Holy shit!"

Shane reached for his towel, but it was too late. It fell onto the rooftop. He was half hard and completely exposed.

Rocco didn't betray any surprise. "That's damn big; I'll give you that."

Ashe said, "I think he's got you beat."

Rocco frowned. "Only one way to find out." He handed Shane the towel. "We need you to come down to the station to get some questions answered for us."

THE COPS

The Central police station was a cesspool of drunks, pimps, hookers, thieves, murderers, and drug addicts. Shane had never been in a police station before. He'd always been a good kid, even in the foster system. The first assault on his senses was the smell. It was a mixture of compost, three-day-old urine, and unwashed body odor.

Rocco steered Shane into a clean room that smelled like Fabuloso and Pine Sol. It masked the odor from outside the door, but it wasn't pleasant.

Ashe came in with a cassette recorder.

Shane said, "Am I in any trouble?"

Both cops laughed. "No, no. The cassette recorder is just for show." Ashe locked the door. "They won't bother us."

Shane pointed to a large square mirror. "There's nobody behind that?"

Rocco lifted the mirror off the wall and put it on the table. "We might need this later."

They were in a windowless room. Shane was scared. Rocco put a hand on his ass. "Easy, guy. We're both queer like you. This is just to settle a bet."

Without ceremony, Rocco pulled down his tight,

dark blue polyester pants, revealing a cock to rival Shane's. "Now it's your turn."

Shane blushed. He was still sure something terrible was about to happen. The woodworker stood, unbuckling his belt. He let his pants drop to his ankles. The monster swung between his legs.

Ashe said, "It's too close to call." He pulled a nightstick from his belt. "Use this to measure."

Rocco grinned. "I don't think that's big enough. Let's use the mirror. We can see who's thicker using the belt."

Ashe took off his belt. His bulbous ass kept his pants from sliding. He put the belt next to the mirror.

Rocco said, "I need a little visual aid. Ashe, pull your pants down."

The handsome brown-haired cop hiked his pants down over his ass, revealing a meaty pair of butt cheeks.

"Spread 'em, stupid."

Ashe held them apart, revealing a sloppy loose hole.

Rocco winked at Shane. "I did that." He hefted his heavy cock with both hands and began stroking. Ashe stretched further, then put a finger in the hole to open it wider. It gaped like a landed carp.

"Oh fuck, yeah!" Rocco elbowed Shane. "Doesn't that look hot?"

Shane had to agree. He was getting hard looking at Rocco, but Ashe's ass was just as exciting. The two men jerked their cocks until they were hard. Rocco flopped his cock next to the mirror, making an indentation with this thumbnail to mark the length.

Shane did the same. He was half an inch longer.

"Fuck!" Rocco was mad. "Maybe I wasn't all the way hard. Nobody is bigger than me!"

He grabbed the belt, tightening it around the thickest part of his shaft. Again, he scratched the leather with his thumbnail, then handed it to Shane.

Shane's circumference was half an inch less than Rocco's.

"Ha! I got you beat, bro. And if you're good at math, you'd know that means I'm bigger than you."

Shane said, "I suck at math. I'll take your word for it."

There was a long silence while the two men sized each other up. The air crackled with a static charge.

Ashe said, "Not here, Rocco."

Rocco grinned. "It wouldn't be the first time."

"But it could be the last!" Ashe folded his arms and glared.

Rocco put his cock away with a sheepish look. "Go ahead, put it away."

Shane wished he wore stretchy polyester police blues like Rocco and Ashe. His Levi's were too tight for his cock to fit when it was still half-hard.

Rocco reached over. "Here, let an expert help you." He artfully maneuvered Shane's cock down one leg.

Ashe said, "We're off duty as of ten minutes ago. Rocco's got a nice pad in Van Nuys. You should come over."

Shane smiled. "I'd like that."

❧

ROCCO'S APARTMENT NEAR THE VAN NUYS CIVIC Center was a palace. It had three bedrooms, two baths, and a huge balcony overlooking the San Fernando Valley.

"I got this place when I worked at the Valley Division. He pointed down from the balcony into the Civic Center, where the police station sat under trees at one end of the plaza. "Central is a pain in the ass commute, but that's where they need me. I met Ashe when we were stationed in Venice. That commute was a nightmare. The 405 is a parking lot."

Shane wasn't entirely at ease yet, so he continued with the small talk. "Where do you live, Ashe?"

"I'm in El Sereno. How about you?"

"Just plain LA, I guess."

The two cops laughed. "There is no "LA," just neighborhoods. Which neighborhood?"

Shane shrugged. "Palms? Mar Vista? I'm not really sure."

Rocco said, "So over by Culver City, yeah?"

Shane nodded. "Yeah, West Side."

Rocco took off his shirt and pulled Shane close. "I bet you like getting fucked. So does Ashe."

Shane relaxed into the cop's arms. "Yeah, I do."

Rocco pulled down Shane's jeans. He bent Shane over a sofa and knelt, licking his hole. The mustache tickled. Shane relaxed and let the cop do his best work.

Ashe climbed on the sofa, putting his loose ass flaps in Shane's face. Shane was fascinated by the way they hung like pussy lips. Ashe was half girl, it seemed. He nibbled on a loose flap, working his tongue in the man's hole. Shanee was getting hard. His cock was trapped against the back of the sofa. Rocco pulled on it like a cow udder, milking it, making it swell and stretch.

The swarthy cop whistled. "I ain't seen a guy this big, except myself, of course."

Shane's mouth was full of loose ass. He slobbered and slurped, causing Ashe to purr like a kitten.

The progression was natural. Rocco sat on the couch, holding his long fat pole upright. Shane sat down on it, gasping with pain as it wriggled inside him, finding the sweet spot and passing it by a mile.

"Ow, fuck!"

Rocco put his hands under Shane's ass, attempting to lift him.

"No," Shane said, "I'm almost there."

Shane's craving for a bigger and bigger dick was finally satisfied. Rocco was thicker than him and nearly as long! The head pushed through the sigmoid colon and struck the descending colon with force. Shane shivered. His cock swelled and rose from the intense pleasure and thrill of being so wholly stuffed with Rocco's magnificent meat.

Then things got interesting. Rocco held Shane by the waist and lifted him to his feet. Ashe lay on the vacated sofa with his legs in the air. Rocco pushed forward until Shane's cock slid over Ashe's sizeable soft penis onto his belly. Rocco pulled back, and Ashe grabbed the head, maneuvering Shane into his hole. With a strong push, Rocco forced Shane into Ashe, who howled with pain and pleasure.

"Oh, sweet Jesus! Oh, Shane, you're so thick! I've never been stretched so wide!"

Ashe's feet kicked the air involuntarily as he spasmed with joy. Soon, the Shane sandwich was ready. Rocco thrust hard. His thrusts reverberated through Shane into Ashe, whose guts began to churn and spasm, caressing Shane's monstrous cock with peristaltic waves.

Now it was Shane's turn to howl. "Oh, fuck! Oh, sweet mother of God!" The blasphemous exhortations didn't begin to describe the intense pleasure Shane felt. He'd never been fucked so deep. Charlie had taken his cock, but Ashe did more. He stroked it with his contractions and belly muscles. The lump in Ashe's belly swelled as Shane grew and swelled bigger and stiffer than he'd ever been. With a cock like his, the extra blood left his head, making him feel faint. He swooned but regained strength as the body drew blood from other regions to feed his overwhelmed brain.

Rocco said, "Fuck, I want you inside me so badly!"

Shane assumed he was talking to Ashe. He wasn't.

Rocco sighed. "I've never been fucked by someone as big as me."

Ashe said, "Yeah, baby, I'd like to see that!"

Until this point, Ashe had remained soft. With Rocco's words, he got a powerful erection. Shane felt it grow and press against his belly. He glanced down and gasped. Ashe was a definite grower and thicker than the other two. Shane wondered what it would be like to be stretched so wide.

Ashe's contractions were contagious. Soon, Shane's guts grabbed hold of Rocco's cock and stroked it.

Rocco blew a hard breath on Shane's neck. "Oh, fuck yeah! Shane, we found our unicorn. Shane's a stroker!"

Ashe wriggled and grinned. "I can't wait."

As the combined weight of Rocco and Shane pressed Ashe's cock into his belly, a steady flow drooled from his piss slit. Shane felt the sticky precum on his stomach. He reached down and took a taste of the salty-sweet brew.

Ashe said, "You like my pussy juice?"

Shane nodded, so overcome with ecstasy he lost the power of speech.

Rocco was first. "Oh, man, I think I'm gonna blow." He sped up, pounding Shane hard. Unlike the little guy at the baths, Shane's guts could take a real beating. It moved him closer to orgasm.

Rocco cursed and cried out. "Here it comes! Fuck! Fuck! I'm gonna come!"

Shane felt Rocco's balls slide over his butt cheeks as they contracted. He felt Rocco's monstrous cock pulse like a bee stinger before the warm flow finally reached the tip and shot into Shane's colon. He counted twelve pulses before it subsided. Rocco must have left a teacup of cum up there.

Rocco continued to hump Shane, still hard as a rock.

Ashe was next. "Oh man, here it comes!" The friction of Shane's belly against Ashe's cock, combined with the incredible stretch in his guts, was enough to push him over the edge. The pressure against his cock was like a thumb over a garden hose. Ashe's cum sprayed everywhere, soiling the couch and the rug behind it, splattering Shane's crotch and thighs.

The warm cum against his thick cock was the clincher. Shane boiled over, his balls pulling up tight. He came like he'd never come before. His balls emptied into Ashe's belly over and over again. Ashe's head thrashed from side to side.

Ashe said, "Oh god! Oh, fuck you're huge!" Then he fainted.

Rocco pulled out of Shane carefully, making sure his colossal cock head pressed against Shane's prostate. When it flopped out, it landed against his knee with a slap. Shane tried to hold back the river, but it trickled and then poured out of him. The sperm stained the carpet as it puddled between Shane's legs.

As Shane withdrew from Ashe, the younger cop revived. "I don't want to let you go." He squeezed in vain, trying to hold Shane inside, but it was too late. From his crouched position, Shane's long cock exited the cop and hit the carpeting. The impact sent a few more drops of cum flying out of his pee hole. He leaned down and lapped up his own cum as it poured out of Ashe's loose flaps. He'd never done anything so depraved, but it felt right. He'd done enough damage to Rocco's flat. He wanted to keep clean what he could.

Rocco brought out a box. "Do you wanna do some coke? We got this off a dealer we busted at Clifton's Cafeteria."

Inside the box was a pile of white powder. Rocco tapped it out onto the glass coffee table with a box-cutting razor. He drew up six lines. Shane was scared. He'd never done drugs, except a bit of marijuana with Charlie and Nasir. He didn't know what to expect.

Ashe went first, sniffing one line in each nostril with a rolled-up twenty. He shook his head.

"Fuck, this is good shit."

Shane leaned down and took two sniffs. He scarcely remembered what came next. Rocco took his hit, and they all began chattering. Rocco played with his limp cock. When he walked to the liquor cabinet for whiskey, his cock bounced off his knees.

Shane felt an intense desire for these two men. It may have been the drugs, but Shane felt like they had known each other their whole lives. He nestled his head in the crouch of Rocco's arm while Ashe massaged his feet. This was bliss. As he crashed off the coke, he grew sleepy. The next thing he knew, it was morning, and Rocco was making pancakes. Before Shane left, Ashe gave him a business card. "Call anytime."

❧ 13 ❧

SHAMUS DIGS BIG

When Shane got home, Nasir was already in the workshop, gluing and clamping chair legs to the seats.

Nasir said, "Where were you? Charlie was ready to start phoning hospitals. You'd better call his work and tell him you're home."

Shane dreaded that call. He didn't want to talk to Nick the Dick or Charlie. He despised Nick, and he felt too guilty to talk to Charlie.

Shane said, "I tell you what. You call Charlie, and I'll take over."

Nasir shrugged. "You're gonna have to talk to him eventually, but okay."

Shane heaved a sigh of relief.

When Charlie got home, he was furious. "You had me worried sick. Where the fuck were you?"

Shane had thought about it. He gave him his best lie. "When I was at the post office, I ran into an old friend from high school and his wife. We got drunk, and I fell asleep on his couch. I'm sorry I didn't call. How was the Dodger's game?"

Charlie laughed. "We spent more time in the bathroom than watching the game. Nasir's cock is like honey, and those Dodger fans are like flies."

Nasir grinned sheepishly. "I couldn't keep them off it. We fucked and sucked all afternoon."

Shane might have felt jealous, but after having had the best sex of his life, he shrugged it off.

The three lovers ate a silent Sunday brunch. The air crackled with resentment and disdain. When Shane put ketchup on his roast beef, Charlie bristled.

"Lay off the fucking ketchup."

At that moment, Shane knew it was over. His mind switched into moving mode. His thoughts raced. He had a whole workshop to relocate. He had nowhere to go. If he broke up with Charlie, he also broke up with his employee Nasir. Would he lose him?

Shane dreaded the conversation. Charlie was the first man who could take him, and Shane was eternally grateful to him. But Charlie was too controlling, and now he was pushing Shane away in favor of the young, pretty Nasir. With Ashe and Rocco, he'd caught a glimpse of a balanced three-way relationship. Both guys could handle a big cock in their ass, not just one. All three were hung very well. Shane absently put his hand in his pocket and felt the business card Ashe gave him. It felt like a ticket to a better life.

❧

SHANE PLANNED HIS MOVE IN SECRET SO THAT HE would be prepared when the time came to break up. He knew it would risk hurting Charlie's feelings, but it was nothing compared to Shane's pain of being shut out of the relationship. Nasir and Charlie planned vacations, went hiking, and even tried scuba diving off Catalina without inviting Shane. The sex grew more infrequent. Shane had to take action.

He called Ashe.

"Hello, Hollenbeck."

"Uh, Ashe?"

There was a long pause. "Shane? Where the fuck have you been? We're dying to do that again."

That evening, while Nasir and Charlie went to the movies, Shane drove over the 405 and met the two men in Van Nuys at Rocco's flat.

Rocco answered the door in a custom leather jockstrap made to hold his gargantuan meat. It must have taken half a cow to get enough leather for the job. Ashe wore a 2XL jockstrap modified with a medium waist. The sight of the two handsome cops dressed for sex made Shane swell in his jeans.

Rocco said, "We got a surprise for you." He ushered Shane into the bedroom. Hanging from the ceiling were two leather hammocks with stirrups. One dangled from the ceiling, empty, but the other was occupied by a compact bodybuilder with a perfect ass and tiny penis.

"Shane, meet Shamus. We hooked up in Venice a few years ago. He's bottomless."

The bodybuilder wriggled and lifted his head to see Shane. "Hey. They tell me you're hung like Rocco. My ass has been twitching ever since."

Rocco patted Shamus on the ass. "What do you think? He's not a lightweight like Hogan. He won't rip in two."

Shamus nodded. "I dig big."

Shane felt a stirring in his loins. The bronzed bodybuilder's teeth were bright white in contrast to his tanned complexion. The tiny penis turned him on, too. Something was exciting about the disparity of nature, where one man could be a hundred times bigger than another.

Rocco tossed Shane a tube of cocoa butter lotion. "Shamus is slicked up inside, but you'd better be sure your dong is greased up, too."

Shane dropped his pants, feeling the monster grow hard and lift off his knees. He held the cock in front of his chest and squeezed the tube of tropical lotion onto the head. He worked it downward.

Shamus looked up and said, "Holy fucking shit. That's thicker than Rocco!"

The Italian cop defended himself. "I'm longer, though."

Shamus said, "A long cock is great. A long, thick cock is awesome."

Shamus had that surfer dude accent that Shane liked so much. He stroked the length of his shaft, reapplying cocoa butter several times until the whole length was slippery.

Shamus wriggled with anticipation in the sling. His tiny dick was already dribbling precum, and Shane hadn't started yet.

Ashe climbed into the sling beside Shamus. He grinned at Shane. "Taking turns, double dicking. You excited?"

Shane was. He smiled. "What does it look like." Indeed, his cock was throbbing and waving in the air. He walked forward until his cock touched Shamus's leg. Shamus extended a muscular arm with huge biceps and triceps and grabbed the head. It slipped out of his hand. Shane took another step forward, so Shamus could guide him into his hole.

At the same time, Rocco pressed his head against Ashe's hole. The two friends were much more familiar with each other's anatomy, and the head slipped in easily.

Ashe gave a great sigh. "Oh, fuck. I'll never get used to that."

Rocco laughed and took a big step forward. Ashe shrieked.

Shamus, meanwhile, had a firm grasp on Shane's massive cock head. Shane's whole body tingled at the touch of the strong, small hand. Shamus steered Shane's cock to his hole and forced the tip past the first sphincter. Shane could feel it lodge in the bodybuilder's hole, which hung loose and sloppy with big, grey pussy lips.

"I use it a lot." Shamus grinned. "It's my thing."

Shane didn't know why it felt so different with Shamus. His skin was soft, despite the enormous muscles. It made Shane's knees feel weak. He leaned forward until the massive head poked past the inner sphincter and slid past Shamus's prostate gland.

The bodybuilder shivered. "Oh, fuck, that's thick."

Shane took a step forward. The leather sling moved away from him. He reached forward and grabbed Shamus's legs to hold him steady as he pushed all the way to the back of the rectum. Shamus groaned. With a loud 'pop,' Shane felt his head rush past the inner junction into the sigmoid colon.

Shamus pounded his chest and cried out like Tarzan. "Holy fucking shit! That thing is a fucking cannon!" It wasn't a complaint. It was genuine joy and lust that fueled Shamus as he screamed.

Shane loved feeling admired. To be valued by a man as perfect as Shamus was a big turn-on. His cock throbbed with desire.

He continued his forward assault, quickly reaching the end of the sigmoid colon. Shamus was short, and so were his insides. Shane was nearly in. He touched the wall of the descending colon, and Shamus lost it.

"Fuck! Fuck! Oh god, fuck me!"

Shane obeyed. He rocked his hips slowly at first, then increased the pace. He looked over and saw Rocco doing the same. Ashe moaned softly, pinching Rocco's teats. The two men were synchronized. As Shane increased his pace, so, too, did Rocco. In a minute or two, they were jackrabbiting.

Shamus threw his head from side to side, writhing in ecstasy. His muscles rippled, finally revealing Shane's cockhead through the thick abdominal wall. Shamus put a hand on the lump and groaned.

Shane could see a similar but much more pronounced lump in Ashe's belly. Ashe was taller, but his body was thin. The bump looked huge. Rocco eyed it proudly. He said, "I never get tired of seeing that, Ashe."

Ashe moaned, thrashing from side to side. His hands formed fists as he punched the air beside him in time to Rocco's high-speed fucking. Shane's excitement doubled, watching the two men beside him give each other so much pleasure.

Shamus's abdominal muscles began to contract involuntarily, massaging Shane's cock more powerfully than anyone had done before. The bodybuilder started to bend at the waist in rapid jerks. He was in the throes of internal orgasm. His tiny penis leaked a fountain of precum. It spilled down his inner thighs and landed on the floor beneath him. Shane caught a drop and licked it off his finger. The hormones were powerful. Shamus's body fluids were like a shot of testosterone cypionate. Shane bent and licked the sweat from his belly, moving downwards until he was licking the tiny nub of a penis. He felt powerful as the hormones dissolved on his tongue. It caused his cock to swell in response.

"Ow! Oh, fuck! I'm gonna burst!" Shamus writhed as he shook with an internal orgasm.

Shane said, "Am I hurting you? Do you want me to stop?"

Shamus said, "Yes, you're hurting me. No, don't stop. I won't break."

Another minute of rapid fucking brought Shamus to male orgasm. He ejaculated in a massive spray of warm cum that hit Shane in the face, the chest, and the crotch. Shamus was covered in cum, too.

"Small gun, plenty of bullets." The bodybuilder grinned.

Seeing that display of hands-free ejaculation put Shane over the edge.

"Oh, shit, Shamus, I'm gonna cum."

Shamus squirmed in anticipation. "Do it, dude. Cum in me."

Shane's head throbbed with desire. His eyesight went red. He'd never felt like this with anyone, not even Charlie. Maybe it was the hormones from Shamus's precum or the soft, muscular skin, but something was different. It felt so good; Shane trembled with desire.

He heard Rocco next to him say, "Get ready. Here it comes."

Ashe jerked his modestly oversized cock vigorously. At the exact moment Shane felt his balls tighten, Ashe shot a massive load. Shamus bucked and belted out a second helping of hands-free cum. Shane felt the warm river taking the long journey up and out of his cock. He flooded Shamus with his seed. Shamus thrashed, then bent forward until his arms surrounded Shane's neck. The two men kissed, and Shane buzzed with a light-headed desire he didn't recognize. He never wanted to stop kissing this incredibly strong little man. He put his hands under Shamus's waist and lifted him, impaled on his cock, and carried him around the bedroom, still hard and ready for another round.

He held the perfect Valentine-shaped buttocks and lifted them, letting them drop hard so that Shamus grunted as the cock hit a spot deep in his insides. He repeated the lift and fall over and over again.

Shamus said, "Dude, you should go into powerlifting." Shamus wrapped his small, powerful legs around Shane's waist and used them to hump the mighty pole inside him. Shane sat on the edge of the bed and lay back with Shamus on top of him. The bodybuilder used his knees as leverage to fuck himself on Shane's huge cock.

Shamus said, "Oh shit, I'm gonna cum again." In another blast, the rich semen sprayed from his tiny penis, landing on Shane's face and open mouth. The taste was exquisite, and the tingling sensation was intoxicating.

Shane's balls pulled up tight without warning, and he blasted another load into Shamus's guts. He yelled with lust and astonishment in equal measure.

"Holy fuck, dude, that was fast."

Shane heard applause nearby. Ashe and Rocco stood, watching the show, their hard cocks standing at attention.

Shamus pointed to Ashe. "You, get in here." He leaned forward over Shane, presenting his stuffed bottom to the cop. Ashe stepped forward and shoved his cock hard. The bodybuilder's ass stretched but didn't give.

Shamus snapped his fingers. Rocco produced a vial of amyl nitrite, which Shamus sniffed deeply. Suddenly, Ashe slid into the gaping stuffed hole.

"Holy shit." Ashe couldn't believe he could fit. He thrust his cock alongside Shane's, enjoying the sensation of two different men encircling his cock, one with his insides, the other with his massive dick.

Shane was surprised to feel his softening cock change directions and swell from the rubbing sensation. Ashe's strokes along the top of his cock were enough to move him forward on a trip toward a third orgasm. Rocco stood by the side of the bed and put the tip of his cock in Shane's mouth. The construction worker nursed on the fat head but couldn't fit it into his mouth.

Rocco said, "Oh fuck, keep doing that." He jerked his massive meat with both hands.

Shamus turned beet red, then another load of cum flooded out of him onto Shane's belly. He began to twist and jerk in the throes of an ass orgasm. His movements caused Ashe to speed up, rubbing against Shane faster and faster. At the same time, Shamus thrust his butt up and down, stroking the two fat cocks with his stretched asshole.

Ashe said, "Oh fuck, I'm gonna cum!" A slippery stream of cum coated Shane's cock, as Shamus pounded up and down. It was all too much. When Rocco let loose a monster load of cum into his mouth, Shane went over. He shouted, "Fuck! I'm cumming again!" And he did. Over and over, he throbbed and squirted, filling Shamus so much that cum began to spray out of his incredibly taut hole.

When Shane and Ashe softened, Shamus's powerful muscles pushed the two cocks out. What looked like a pint of cum poured out of his asshole. Shane swallowed Rocco's load, licking his lips.

❧ 14 ❧

NEW LOVE

The four naked men returned to the living room and sat on the sofa.

"Drinks? Cocaine?" Ashe stood by the bar, holding up a bottle of Tequila.

Shamus said, "Nah. My body is a temple. I don't do any of that stuff anymore."

Shane stared at him admiringly. Shamus caught his eye and stretched, placing his hands behind his head and flexing his biceps. Shane was awestruck by how sexy this compact, handsome man could be. His pectoral muscles still glistened with sweat from the vigorous sex.

"How about you, Shane. Some joy powder?"

Shane shrugged. "Nah, I don't really do that stuff either." He wanted to impress Shamus. It worked.

The Irish bodybuilder said, "You got the kind of body that buffs up nice. I'm glad you take care of it."

Rocco looked from one man to the other. "I think you two dig each other."

Shamus blushed. "Yeah, he's cool." He winked at the woodworker.

Shane said, "I'd do him."

They all laughed at the absurd comment.

Shamus said, "I wanna blow Ashe with you two up my ass."

His straightforward delivery was hot. Shane felt his thrice-spent cock lift in anticipation of a fourth orgasm.

Shane asked, "How will that work?"

It took a lot of thought, but Shane and Rocco figured out how to sit sideways, facing one another on the sofa, each one's legs stretched past the other's waist. They scooted until their balls touched. Shamus stood on the edge of the couch and squeezed the two humongous cock heads together, sitting on them like a barstool. He put his full weight on the coffee-can-sized bundle until the two tips entered him, then wedged in place.

"Fuck! Fuck! I want it so bad!" Shamus wriggled and bounced, trying to fit the impossibly large payload in his ass. With help from Rocco and Shane, who held his bottom, he lifted his legs. That kept him aloft, so they could slowly lower him an inch at a time once he finally loosened up. Shamus took a massive hit off the bottle of poppers, and his poop chute relaxed. He dropped an inch, then two, until the two heads entered the rectum completely.

Shamus let out a huge breath. "God damn! I thought it couldn't be done. He lowered his legs and sat down further, pushing the two cocks to the tight junction. Again he sat on the two men's hands, legs outstretched, letting gravity help force the cock heads past his inner hole.

Ashe watched in morbid fascination, occasionally stroking his cock, which hung half hard at his thigh. When there was a loud hand-clap sound, Shamus squealed like a pig. Ashe felt the blood rush to his cock, knowing that his two friends had passed the junction. Shamus put his feet back on the sofa's edge, now bent at a 90-degree angle. He stepped off the edge of the couch with one leg, forcing the meat deeper inside him. When the other foot hit the floor, Shamus was three inches from the base of the two cocks. He bent his waist, a strange ripple forming across his abdomen. It was the outline of the two elephantine cocks stretching him beyond the limits. He sat down all the way, jerking when the two cocks hit the descending colon.

Shane immediately felt the involuntary contractions of Shamus's powerful abdominal muscles. He couldn't see Shamus's face, but he imagined the eyes rolling up in the back of his head.

Shamus pulled Ashe forward, clamping his mouth on his cock. Ashe thrust his hips, hitting the back of Shamus's throat. The bodybuilder retched, which made the contractions in his guts double in speed. His head bobbed up and down, taking more and more of Ashe's cock in his throat until it reached the esophagus. There, Shamus held Ashe's ass and pushed him in further. Shane could see the root of the cock disappear in Shamus's mouth. It turned him on.

Shamus raised and lowered his hips with his powerful glutes, stroking both men lodged so firmly inside him. He pulled back and gasped for air, then swallowed Ashe whole again.

Rocco took Shane's hand and squeezed. The connection was there, but it was Shamus whose heady scent and perfect buttocks linked all three men together. His mouth completed the circuit with Ashe.

Rocco was the first. He'd only come twice. "Fuck, man, I'm gonna cum."

Shamus sped up his bouncing, his abdominal muscles bulging with each downward thrust. Ashe watched the bodybuilder's stomach distend. He said, "That's so fucking hot."

Thin trickles of sweat coursed down Shamus's body. Shane leaned forward and licked the musky perspiration from his perfect little body. He put a hand on Shamus's tiny penis, rubbing it until it produced a payload of precum. He slurped the precum, licking his fingers and swooning from the taste.

Rocco threw his head back. "I'm coming! Motherfuck!" The cop's sperm had nowhere to go but up the descending colon. Shane felt it rain back down on his cockhead in warm cupfuls. Shamus wriggled, moaning softly.

Ashe was next. "God damn, you give good head. I'm gonna fucking come."

Shamus pulled the cock out of his mouth long enough to say, "Do it." Then he went all the way down until Ashe's pubic hair tickled his nose. Ashe's breath grew heavy. "It's fucking coming. It's coming. Aargh!"

Shane could hear the effluence gurgling in Shamus's throat. It sounded like a small brook running over rocks, but it was semen squeezing past the Adam's apple and down the bodybuilder's throat. Shamus swallowed every last drop.

Shane's cock was struggling. He'd emptied his balls three times already. A fourth orgasm would take a long time. But Rocco put a finger in Shane's ass and played with it. He pressed on Shane's prostate, which acted like a panic button. Suddenly, he felt renewed strength. His cock throbbed against Rocco's huge soft beast, still wedged tightly in the bodybuilder's entrails. He felt Rocco harden from the pressure.

Shamus planted one of Shane's hands on his massive chest and directed him to play with his nipple. Shane squeezed and rubbed it, feeling an electric current running down his arm and into his belly. Shamus must have felt it, too, because the contractions increased threefold until Shamus was a milking machine, sure to squeeze out one last load from Shane's enormous cock. Rocco was throbbing again, which created sine waves of pleasure in harmony with Shamus's rhythmic muscle spasms.

Shamus took Shane's other hand and placed it on his penis. "Rub my clit."

The words were so powerful Shane felt another ejaculation begin to form.

Rocco said, "Shit, man, I think I'm gonna cum again."

Both men climaxed at the same time. Rocco spilled another biblical flood of cum up Shamus's bum, and Shane exploded, packing Shamus's descending colon with cupfuls of cum. The little bodybuilder shook and came in Shane's cupped hand, filling it to overflowing. Shane brought it to his lips and sipped the heady elixir. He grew dizzy at the taste.

When Shamus stood, the two giant soft cocks were still wedged inside him pretty far. He climbed onto the couch to extract them from his guts. Each fell with a loud 'thwack' onto the other's thigh. They were followed by loud farts of cum that stained the couch and coated both men's legs and cocks. Shamus collapsed on Shane's chest, tracing circles around his nipples. "I know I can make you grow. Will you let me train you?"

Shane nodded. "I'd love that."

15

GOLD'S GYM

The following Monday, Shane joined Shamus at Gold's Gym in Venice. The Mecca of body-building was ground zero for hot guys. Most were too interested in lifting to notice Shane's bulging sweatpants, but a few heads turned and tilted downward in surprise. Shamus stood between the hungry eyes and his companion in a protective stance.

"We're gonna start easy with the chest. You look like you could press 60 pounds right now."

Shane asked, "How much can you lift?"

Shamus shrugged. "On a good day, 250."

Shane felt embarrassed to be so weak. Shamus anticipated the emotion. "Don't compare yourself to anyone but yourself. Keep at this; you'll be over 100 in no time."

After four cycles of ten lifts, they moved on to the Preacher Curl. Shane was surprised when his biceps responded, growing before his eyes.

Shamus said, "The biceps are amazing. They respond right away."

After they completed an entire body circuit, Shane felt like one giant bruise. His muscles ached, his joints hurt, and he hunched over.

Shamus patted his rump. "Don't worry. The first day is the worst. It gets better and better."

The gym filled with whispers. One huge bodybuilder with a feminine voice approached. "Shane and Shamus, what a cute name for a couple. Is that thing real?" The queeny hulk pointed to Shane's crotch.

Shane was appalled by the rudeness. Shamus stood up, hormones raging. "Fuck off, Gary Mary. We're not a couple."

Shane surprised himself by saying, "Not yet."

Gary Mary walked away in a snit. Shamus turned to him. "What did you mean by not 'yet'?"

Shane shrugged. "I don't know. It just slipped out."

Shamus broke into a smile. "It's only our second date."

Shane said, "This is a date?"

Shamus laughed. "To me, it is. I never fuck on a second date, but for you, I might make an exception. Now, let's hit the showers."

The shower heads were lined up with no barriers. Men of all shapes and sizes stood in the showers, some playing with themselves, others focused on cleaning their sweat-soaked muscles. There were audible gasps when Shane stripped off his sweats and hung them on a nearby hook. Heads turned, and whispers filled the air.

Shamus glared, but the eyes remained fixed. The men shuffled forward like moths to a flame, hoping to touch the magnificent beast.

There were too many hands for Shane to slap away, so Shamus helped him. In a final move, he picked up Shane's cock and shoved it partway in his ass. It was the only way to keep the hands at bay. More gasps. Nobody could believe it fit.

"He's mine, motherfuckers, so back off!"

Shane swelled and stretched, excited by Shamus's masculine behavior and feminine receptivity.

The Irishman laughed. "You're hard, ain't you. I

can't let them see that." He backed toward Shane, taking more and more of the obscenely large cock in his backside. The gasps became cries of wonder. When Shane's cock poked out from Shamus's belly, the air filled with astonishment.

"Holy shit."

"I can't believe it."

"So fucking hot, dude."

There wasn't a soft cock in the showers. Every man, even the straight assholes, was playing with himself. Shamus shook and jerked, stroking Shane with his belly from the inside. Shane groaned with satisfaction. He yearned to come inside his new friend.

One by one, the men in the shower began to pop off. The cum flew skyward until the shower room rained with manly essence. The smell of the locker room was musky and strong. It put Shane over the precipice.

"Oh Fuck, Shamus, I'm coming."

"Me, too." Sure enough, Shamus's tiny penis shot a massive load of cum on the floor. Shane caught some and put it in his mouth, savoring the perfectly masculine stew. It sent him over. His balls pulled tight, gurgling with semen, and his cock pulsed like a bee stinger, shooting ropes of cum inside Shamus's beautiful ass.

When he was done, he pulled back. His softening cock hit his knee, causing the room to gasp at the impressive size. There was a round of applause before everyone returned to the shower.

16

NEW LOVE

Shamus and Shane's performance backfired. Gold's Gym management started an "anti-sex" campaign. Signs went up stating that members found engaging in sexual activity would have their membership revoked and would be permanently banned from the gym. Since Gold's was a second home to Shamus, he obeyed and asked Shane not to shower there, as it would inevitably lead to sex. His cock was just too powerful.

One afternoon, when they left the gym so Shane could shower at Shamus's bachelor pad, they passed a "For Lease" sign on a warehouse near Paloma and South Main St. A lightbulb went off. Shane said, "I wonder if they have living quarters." Shamus knocked on the door. A wizened old man opened the door.

"How can I help you, Sonny?"

Shamus asked the old fellow if someone could live there.

"I live here now. I'm moving back to Kansas."

Venice was a bit of a dump, so the price was reasonable. Shane wanted to get away from Charlie and Nasir. He saw his chance. He put the money down and moved his workshop to Venice.

The breakup went very smoothly. Nasir was ready to

take over his father's business and no longer wanted to build furniture. Charlie had tired of Shane and wanted to be exclusive with Nasir. So when Shane made the announcement, everyone breathed a collective sigh of relief. Shane would have to find a new apprentice, but he figured the right person would make themselves known.

He started to spread the word among the bodybuilders at the gym. Shamus overheard and approached him. "Hey, I'm barely scraping by on unemployment. How much does the apprenticeship pay?"

Shane had never considered Shamus, who spent so much of his days at the gym. His barrel chest and strong legs would go a long way to help load furniture. He would make a good fit if he had an eye for detail, which was the big unknown.

Like Nasir, Shane started Shamus turning wood. He was unusually good at it.

"Did you learn to do this before?"

Shamus nodded. "I took woodshop in high school. And my father was a woodcarver."

Shane was stunned. Their friendship was so focused on bodybuilding and fucking, they never discussed the details of their lives.

The living quarters were nice. There was a loft above the workshop with a big bedroom, a kitchen, and a full bath. Shane traded in his twin bed for a California King. He and Shamus fucked on that bed every waking hour that they weren't working out, eating, or building furniture. The kissing grew more intense until, at last, one afternoon, Shamus whispered, "I love you, Shane."

It was a watershed moment. Shane pushed his way in deep, kissing Shamus in earnest. He pulled back. "I love you, too."

They became a couple. At the gym, people referred to the couple as "Shanus." Under Shamus's tutelage, Shane became a massive hunk of muscle. Shane's cock was no longer the first thing people noticed about him. His broad shoulders, bulging biceps, and curvaceous chest drew attention to all the action above the waistline. When their eyes descended, they caught a glimpse of the thick monster hiding in his baggy sweats. Walking down Main Street, the two men turned heads and caused fender benders. At the local gay bar, the Roosterfish, they were stars. If a man was lucky enough to catch their attention, he could bet he was in for a great time back at the warehouse. They went for all types of guys as long as they were handsome. Shane wasn't as particular as Shamus about what dick went in his ass as long as it was long enough to stay in. Shamus could never fill that duty, but it was never a point of contention in the relationship. Shamus was a total bottom by design, and he loved it. Rocco and Ashe sometimes made the commute from the Valley, and the fuck fests would last all night.

The gym was an excellent source of sexual partners for the couple. Shamus lured them home with his bulbous ass. The showers were off-limits for Shane, who always created an outbreak of sex zombies. But Shamus, with his tiny penis and bubble butt, was the perfect bait for the well-hung bodybuilders. When competitions came to town, the gym was filled with exotic lifters from around the world. It was a sexual smorgasbord. Cocks of every shape, size, and color were on the buffet table.

Most encounters began as a show. The men they brought home were incredulous when they saw Shane in full glory. A few thought they could take him, but it was never the case. Instead, they would watch in fascination as Shamus climbed on top and sat down on the long, thick fuckpole. From there, Shane would expose his ass and let the visitor in. There were a hundred variants of the basic situation, but the encounters usually played out just like that.

Going to the Hinano Cafe in Venice, you might see an incredibly handsome bodybuilding couple sitting at the bar, eating burgers. If the short one has a good ass, then take a good look at the tall one. His sawdust-covered hands give him away. If your eyes drop, you'll see something impressive hanging down one leg. If you can peel away your eyes long enough to look at their faces, you'll likely catch them staring at each other with a burning hot love. If you're fortunate, you'll see them talking to a couple of cops. Look closely at the darker one; you'll gasp when your eyes drop below the belt. It's not his nightstick or a trick of the light; it's all very, very real.

ABOUT THE AUTHOR

Peter Schutes is an imaginary gay historical figure with a rich backstory. He was born in the United States in 1896. After a brief study period at Harvard University, he enlisted and fought in World War I. After the war, he was incarcerated at Napa State Mental Hospital because of his homosexuality. When he was released, he came to Hollywood, where he became a hustler.

Arrested for drug dealing, Peter escaped and fled to Kentucky. There, he worked in a coal mine, where he met his first real love. After the death of his lover, Peter retired to a bunkhouse in Montana, where he found an old typewriter and began exploring his fantasies in writing. Eventually, after laws changed, he was able to publish his gay pulp fiction books in Denmark and then the United States.

Peter returned to Los Angeles and lived out his days in the increasingly accepting society of that city. He died in Santa Monica, CA, in 1981. Except Peter Schutes didn't exist. He's a pen name.

OTHER BOOKS FROM PETER SCHUTES PUBLISHING

E-books and Paperbacks (as noted)

The Able Seaman

The Anaconda Copper

The Autobiography of Peter Schutes*

Backwoods Delivery

Big Bodies of All Sizes*

Big Hole River*

Bobbing Buoys and Salty Seamen*

Bunkhouse Buddies*

The Butt Baby*

Cloistered

Confessions of a Rodeo Clown*

Dark as a Dungeon*

Demonic Deception *aka* Deceived, Cursed & Blessed

Desert Island Daddies

The Expectant Member

Firehouse Lovers

The Fish

Five Erotic Tales*

The Gospel of Priapus

Hercules and Lippos

Hobo Honey

Hot Blue Collars*

Hotshot

Logger's Delight

Panama Heat

Satanic Seductions*

Satan's Sissy Boy

The Slaves of Rome*

The Thigh Baby

Under the Boardwalk

World's Biggest

Coming Soon

Backwoods Delivery - The Complete Daddy's Boy Series

Like the Greeks Do*

Higher Education*

Hoboes, Hustlers, and Jailbirds*

Small Cockpits and Big Hangars*

Tales of Two Daddies*

*Available as Paperbacks